POCKET IRISH LEGENDS

Stories retold by Fiona Biggs

Illustrated by Kay Dixey & Lucy Su

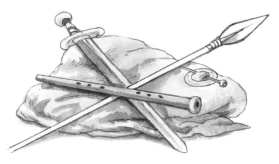

Gill Books

Gill Books
Hume Avenue, Park West, Dublin 12

www.gillbooks.ie

Gill Books is an imprint of M.H. Gill & Co.

Copyright © Teapot Press Ltd 2014

ISBN: 978-0-7171-5899-7

This book was created and produced by Teapot Press Ltd

Edited by Fiona Biggs
Designed by Tony Potter
Additional stories by Felicity Trotman

Printed in EU

This book is typeset in Sabon Infant

A CIP catalogue record for this book is available
from the British Library.

10 9 8 7 6 5

POCKET
IRISH
LEGENDS

Contents

Introduction

The rich and colourful history of Ireland is reflected in the legends and myths that have been handed down from generation to generation over hundreds of years, which are loved by children and adults alike. In the days before most people were able to read or write, the stories were told by travelling storytellers or 'seanchaí', who would go from village to village, receiving bed and board in return for a story or two. Later on, before radio, television or the internet came along and took all our attention, people would sit around the fire during the long winter evenings, telling the old stories. Neighbours would call in to join the story sessions, and each family in a town or village would host the storytelling evenings in turn.

Many of the legends passed down in this way were based on things that had happened in history, and they were centred on people who actually existed. The coming of Christianity, the Viking invasions and the English occupation of Ireland can all be found in these pages. Of course, as the years went by and the stories were told and retold, the tales were embroidered and embellished, and kings of old sometimes grew into giants or were even given magical powers to help them vanquish their enemies. Natural wonders, such as the remarkable absence of snakes in Ireland and the amazingly intricate construction of the Giant's Causeway, were interpreted in the legends of Saint Patrick and the Snakes and Fionn Mac Cumhaill and the Giant from Scotland, in a way that could be understood by people with no knowledge of the natural sciences.

In this book you will find tales of beautiful princesses and handsome princes, brave kings, beautiful queens, wicked stepmothers, greedy landlords, wily druids, practical saints, magic spears, singing harps, huge monsters, slithering snakes, fierce dragons, cruel enchantments, courageous deeds, mischievous fairies and clever leprechauns. There's even a fearless female pirate!

These are stories of courage, love, betrayal, greed, stupidity, magic and miracles. They were a means by which people could escape their daily cares and problems, although a surprising number of the tales are populated by people with exactly the same problems as the eager listeners. Leprechaun gold has always been a great draw for people with hardly any money; of course, the humans are taken for fools and the leprechauns win the day – every time.

The lovely names that many Irish people choose for their children show that there is still a lot of interest in the old tales. All the Deirdres, Aoifes, Conors, Gráinnes, Diarmuids, Brians, Niamhs, Maeves and Oisíns will find themselves in the old legends: Deirdre of the Sorrows, The Pursuit of Diarmuid and Gráinne, Fionn Mac Cumhaill and the Salmon of Knowledge, Oisín in Tír na nÓg, Brian Boru, The Brown Bull of Cooley, The Children of Lir. Just meeting people with these names keeps the old stories alive and connects us with history. 'Where does my name come from?' A question easily answered with a story.

Although fairies appear in many of the stories, these are not simple fairy tales. They are tales that reflect people's deepest emotions and concerns – you will probably even recognise yourself in some of them! People don't always deserve the misfortunes that come their way in these stories, many of which don't have a happy ending – the heart-breakingly sad story of the Children of Lir is a good example of an unhappy tale. But then, life is like that.

With 28 compellingly told and beautifully illustrated stories, there's something in this collection for everyone, young or old, to enjoy.

Fionn Mac Cumhaill and the Salmon of Knowledge

Long ago in Ireland, the high king formed a special army of all his best warriors. The group was known as the Fianna and their job was to protect the king from his enemies. Their leader, the mightiest warrior of them all, was called Cumhall. He was a great favourite of the king and the other warriors were very jealous of him. They plotted against him and, one day, they seized their chance and murdered him. His wife became afraid that her baby son Fionn would also be murdered, so she took him on a dangerous journey to a cave in the Sliabh Bloom Mountains where two women, one a warrior, the other a druid, lived. She asked the women to take care of the boy, to keep him safe and to teach him everything they knew so that he would be able to pass the difficult initiation tests of the Fianna when he came of age.

The women, who were called Bobdal and Fiacal, agreed to look after Fionn. 'We will call him Demne,' they said. 'We will hide him away in such a safe place that even you will not be able to find him.' This was a great sacrifice for Fionn's mother, who loved her son dearly, but she knew that she would have to leave him and entrust him to the women to guarantee his safety from his father's enemies. She made her sad farewells and returned to her home.

As he grew up, Demne learned all the things he would need to admit him to the ranks of the Fianna. The women taught him how to defend himself against the spears of nine warriors using only his shield. He learned how to live in the wild, with only his spear

to help him find enough food to eat. The women also showed him how to make magic spells to defeat his enemies. These were all things that would be very useful to him during his life as a warrior.

An Irish warrior also needed to learn the art of poetry, so, when they had taught him all they knew, the two women sent Demne to study with the old poet Finnéigeas, who lived beside the great River Boyne.

Finnéigeas had made his home beside a deep pool in the river. There was a legend that the Salmon of Knowledge lived in this pool and that the person who caught the salmon and ate it would know everything that there was to know in the world.

One day, Finnéigeas was fishing in the pool with his spear when he suddenly shouted out to Demne, 'Come quickly! I have finally caught the Salmon of

Knowledge!' Demne immediately stopped what he was doing and, under Finnéigeas's instructions, built a fire and made a spit to cook the great fish. 'Whatever you do,' ordered the old man, 'do not allow any of the cooked flesh to touch your mouth. I have waited many years for this moment, and the precious gift of knowledge belongs to me by right.'

Demne cooked the fish very carefully, but when the skin began to form a blister, he reached out to break it. The hot fat burned his thumb and he put it into his mouth to stop the pain. He had just finished cooking the fish when Finnéigeas returned. When the old man looked into Demne's eyes, he knew that the precious gift of knowledge, for which he had waited all his life, had passed to Demne. Then he realised that there was something different about the young man, something that he had not noticed before.

'What is your real name?' he asked. 'My mother called me Fionn, son of Cumhall,' he replied. 'But why do you ask?'

'I can teach you nothing more, Fionn Mac Cumhaill,' said the old man. 'You must go to the king and take your father's place as commander of the Fianna, which is your destiny.'

Fionn thanked Finnéigeas for all he had done for him and set out for the high king's palace at Tara. From that day forward, if he needed to know something, he had only to put his thumb in his mouth for a moment and all was revealed!

Fionn Mac Cumhaill and the Dragon

When Fionn left his teacher, Finnéigeas, he set out for the court of the high king at Tara. The road was thronged with people arriving to join in the great Samhain festivities. Powerful warriors and chieftains were gathering at Tara for the annual celebrations. The great hall was full to overflowing and huge fires were crackling in all the grates. Servants were running to and fro, carrying enormous platters of roasted meat and game to feed all the visitors. Dogs were running around under all the tables looking for scraps. The wine jugs were being filled and refilled and loud laughter filled the air.

When Fionn burst through the doors silence fell and you could have heard a pin drop. There was no seat for him, so he approached the king, watched by all the chieftains and warriors.

'Who are you?' asked the king. 'Who is this stranger who marches in here so boldly?'

'I am Fionn, son of Cumhall,' replied the young man in a clear, proud voice.

'You are welcome here,' said the king. 'Your father was a great friend to me.'

'How may I serve you, my king?' asked Fionn.

'Well,' replied the king, 'There is something you may be able to do for me.' And he started to tell a strange story.

'Every Samhain for the past nine years, Tara has been besieged by an evil spirit in the form of a fire-breathing dragon. When the dragon comes near it plays sweet music, and all who hear it fall into a deep sleep. Many warriors have tried to slay it but have died in the attempt. Our magicians have used spells to destroy the dragon, but they have all failed. If you can save Tara, I will grant you whatever you want.'

'I will slay the dragon for you, my king,' vowed Fionn, and he strode out in the dark night to wait for the beast. Suddenly he heard a soft voice saying, 'Fionn, your father was a good friend to me. I have come to repay a favour your father did for me.' Fionn looked around, but could see no one.

'You cannot see me,' said the voice, 'but look up and you will see a spear.' Fionn looked up and, just above his head, was a beautiful silver spear.

'As you know,' said the voice, 'when the dragon approaches he plays sweet music, and anyone who hears it falls asleep at once. Take the magic spear and press it firmly against your forehead as soon as the music begins. The dragon's music will have no power over you.'

Fionn waited for what seemed like a long time and then he heard a single note being played on a pipe, a note of enchanting sweetness. All the people at Tara fell into a deep sleep, but Fionn pressed the spear to his forehead and the music stopped immediately. He saw the dragon standing before him, his breath on fire, and he hurled the magic spear straight between its eyes. The dragon fell to the ground. Fionn took his sword and cut off its head with a single swing. He took the head, went back into the banquet and presented his trophy to the king, bowing low.

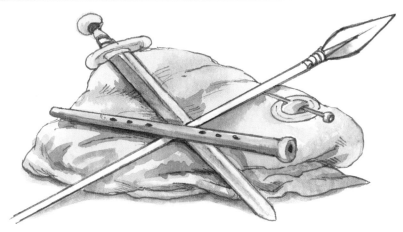

'You have saved us from the dragon,' said the king. 'What is your dearest wish?'

'I ask to be leader of the Fianna, as my father was,' said the hero.

The king gladly granted his wish. All the other warriors submitted to him and that is how Fionn Mac Cumhaill became the greatest leader the Fianna ever had.

Fionn Mac Cumhaill and the Giant from Scotland

Fionn was enjoying a comfortable life with his wife Una in his big castle beside the sea in County Antrim. It was a time of peace, so Fionn was able to take a break from his life as a warrior with the Fianna. To pass the time, he decided to build a broad path across the sea from Antrim to Scotland. It was a very unusual path, made of hundreds of thousands of black rocks, all different sizes, none of them either square or round. Some of the rocks had six sides, some eight and others more than ten.

The warriors of the Fianna looked on in amazement as Fionn worked hard at his task each day. Before

long, his causeway stretched miles into the sea between the two coasts.

One evening, just after he had returned home after a hard day's work, a stranger arrived – a messenger from Scotland just across the sea.

'I bring a challenge from the mighty Angus,' the messenger told Fionn. 'He is the tallest, strongest and most fearsome giant in all Scotland. He has beaten all the other giants in combat but he has heard tales of your great strength and he wants to fight you. Do you accept his challenge?'

'Of course I accept,' said Fionn. 'I will begin to prepare myself immediately.'

However, after the messenger left, Fionn noticed that Una was looking very worried.

'What's the matter?' he asked.

'Oh, Fionn,' she replied. 'I'm not sure that you should have accepted Angus's challenge. I've heard that he's much bigger than you and is definitely stronger.'

Fionn thought about this for a while, then he said, 'If I cannot beat him with my strength, I must think of a plan. I may not be as big or as strong as he is, but I am much, much cleverer.'

Fionn and Una talked for hours, but they couldn't come up with a plan that was clever enough to defeat Angus. Nothing that occurred to them was cunning enough to beat the giant.

Later that week Angus's messenger returned and told Fionn that his master would arrive in two days. Time was running out.

Una said calmly, 'Tell him that Fionn is ready and waiting.'

'Why did you say that?' asked Fionn, when the messenger had gone on his way.

'Don't worry,' replied Una. 'I have a plan in mind. Leave it to me.'

For the next two days Una snipped and sewed and knitted.

'How can you waste time sewing and knitting at a time like this!' bellowed Fionn when he saw what she was doing.

'Look carefully,' said Una. 'What do you see?'

'Clothes,' said Fionn. 'You've been making clothes, baby clothes, but who on earth could they fit? They're absolutely enormous!'

'Never mind that,' said Una. 'Just put them on and be quick about it. We have no time to lose.'

Fionn obediently dressed himself in the clothes she had made. What a sight he was! He wore a long dress, a pair of woolly booties and a lovely knitted bonnet on his head.

'Now, get into that cradle.' Fionn looked around and saw an enormous wooden cradle.

'I asked Fergus to make the cradle while you were working. Now, in you get, quickly; I can hear Angus coming.'

The ground shook with every step the Scottish giant took. When he arrived at the castle he was met by Una.

'Where is the mighty Fionn?' he roared. 'I have come all the way from Scotland to find him. Is he afraid to meet me?'

Una welcomed him in.

'Not at all,' she said. 'You're very welcome. Please come in. Fionn is out hunting at the moment, but he won't be long. I've just got the baby to sleep, so I'd be grateful if you could speak a little more softly.'

Angus looked over at the cradle. 'That is your baby?' he asked, shocked, for he had never seen such a large baby.

'Yes, this is our little one,' said Una, glowing with maternal pride. 'We're very proud of him, even though he's rather small for his age, but we hope he'll grow up to be at least as big as his father.'

Angus was suddenly very frightened.

'If this is Fionn's baby, what size can Fionn be?' he wondered. 'He must be absolutely huge!'

He rushed out of the castle and ran across the causeway, back to Scotland. As he was running he suddenly realised that Fionn might be following him, so he turned around and began to remove the stones from the path behind him, so that by the time he arrived back in Scotland there were just a few stones left, jutting out from the coast of Antrim into the sea.

And, to this day, that's all that remains of the giant's causeway.

The Pursuit of Diarmuid and Gráinne

Fionn Mac Cumhaill's wife had died and the leader of the Fianna was looking for a new one. He sent his warriors all around Ireland to find someone suitable. After searching the whole land, they came to the fort of Cormac Mac Airt, the high king of Ireland, and it was there that they first laid eyes on his beautiful daughter, Gráinne.

Although Gráinne had been courted by all the chieftains of Ireland, Cormac had not accepted any of them as a suitable husband for his daughter. When the Fianna asked him to consider Fionn as a prospective groom, he decided that the great warrior would make a worthy husband. The match was made, the bride price was struck, and preparations for a huge wedding feast began. Cattle were counted, guests were invited, and Gráinne's ladies started sewing a beautiful wedding gown for her. The kitchen staff were kept busy from morning until night, preparing a huge feast that would last for days.

Gráinne had never set eyes on Fionn, but she had been told that he was one of the greatest warriors Ireland had ever had and she was nervously looking forward to meeting him. However, when he arrived for the betrothal ceremony, she was dismayed to discover that he was older than her own father. Gráinne was as wilful as she was beautiful, and she decided on the spot that she wouldn't marry Fionn.

'Surely my father does not expect me to marry this old man!' she said to herself, and she went to find Cormac.

'I can't marry Fionn,' she declared. 'He's older than you!'

'You don't have a choice,' said her father. 'The deal has been made and we can't back out of it now without bloodshed. Anyway, you won't find a braver man in all Ireland.'

Gráinne didn't want to dishonour her father, so she attended the betrothal feast, sitting on Fionn's right hand at the high table. From there she had a good view of all the guests and her eyes fell on the handsome Diarmuid, one of Fionn's most trusted and honoured warriors. When Diarmuid looked up from his food she caught his eye and he was smitten with love for her.

The next day, Gráinne was sitting at the window of her chamber, watching a game of hurling. She couldn't help noticing how much faster and more skilled Diarmuid was than all the other players, and she couldn't avoid comparing him to her intended husband.

Although Gráinne knew that Diarmuid was the only man for her, she knew that the only way to stop her wedding to Fionn was to leave before they had taken their vows. This was a problem, because there was going to be another huge feast that night, and the couple would exchange their vows the following day.

Finally, she decided what to do. She knew that Diarmuid would be standing guard that night so he wouldn't be joining the celebrations. She mixed a sleeping potion into the mead served at the feast and soon everyone fell into a deep sleep.

43

Gráinne went outside to find Diarmuid.

'Run away with me, Diarmuid,' she said. 'I can't live without you and I can't marry Fionn.'

However, Diarmuid was completely loyal to Fionn and he refused to leave with her. By now, Gráinne was desperate, so she put a curse on Diarmuid, forcing him to do whatever she wanted. She told him that he must leave with her immediately.

'You shouldn't have done that,' Diarmuid said. 'You're making me betray Fionn and you're bringing dishonour on your father. This is an evil thing you've done and evil will follow us to the end of our days.'

The couple ran away, across the length and breadth of Ireland. When Fionn realised what had happened he set off in hot pursuit. It is said that there was no nook or cranny, no cave or hollow tree trunk where the eloping couple did not hide. They crossed the River Shannon to hide in a wood, they hid in a tree in the wilds of County Galway and they hid in the bracken at Lough Gur in County Limerick.

Fionn came very close to finding them several times. Once, when the Fianna had almost caught up with them, Diarmuid's foster father had to hide them with his cloak of invisibility.

After some years, Fionn got tired of the chase. He said that he had forgiven Diarmuid and was leaving the couple to live in peace. Diarmuid and Gráinne were finally able to settle down to a happy life together.

Years later, Fionn decided one day to go boar hunting near Ben Bulben in County Sligo. Diarmuid joined the chase, even though it had once been prophesied that he would be killed by a boar.

During the hunt Diarmuid was cornered by a boar, and although he managed to kill it eventually, he was badly wounded in the struggle. Fionn and the Fianna found him in the forest, dying from his wounds. They brought him home to Gráinne.

'Please help him,' Gráinne begged Fionn. 'If you give him a drink of water cupped in your magical hands, that will cure him.'

But Fionn was still angry that Diarmuid had run away with his bride, so he refused to help him. Even though the Fianna begged Fionn to save this great warrior of the Fianna, he still refused and Diarmuid died in Gráinne's arms after a few hours. And so, Gráinne knew that her curse had, at last, brought evil on them, as Diarmuid had predicted when she laid it on him. Soon afterwards, she died of a broken heart.

Oisín in Tír na nÓg

One day some of the Fianna were hunting deer on the shores of Loch Léin in Kerry. They saw a beautiful white horse coming towards them, ridden by the most beautiful woman they had ever seen. She was wearing a dress as blue as the sky in summer, studded with silver stars, and her long golden hair hung down to her waist.

'What is your name and where have you come from?' asked Fionn, the leader of the Fianna.

'I have come from Tír na nÓg', replied the woman. 'My father is the king of that land. I am known as Niamh of the Golden Hair.'

'But why have you come here?' asked Fionn.

'I have heard of a warrior called Oisín,' answered Niamh. 'Tales of his courage and poetry have reached our land. I have come to find him and take him back with me to Tír na nÓg.'

'Oisín is my son,' said Fionn proudly. 'And he is indeed a great hero and a poet.'

Oisín came forward and stood before Niamh, entranced by her beauty.

'Tell me,' he asked her, 'what sort of country is Tír na nÓg?'

'Tír na nÓg is the land of youth,' replied Niamh. 'It is a happy place, with no pain or sorrow or death. Any wish you make there comes true and nobody grows old. If you come with me you will see that this is the truth.'

Fionn was sad to think that his son would leave him and the Fianna, and made him promise to come back soon.

'I promise,' said Oisín, as he mounted the white horse behind Niamh. He said goodbye to his father and his friends and the horse galloped away over the water, moving as swiftly as the shadow of a cloud on a windy day. The Fianna were sad to see their hero leave, but Fionn reminded them of Oisín's promise to return soon.

When Oisín and Niamh arrived in Tír na nÓg, the king and queen gave him a warm welcome and held a huge feast in his honour. In the days following the feast, Oisín explored the wonderful land with Niamh and found that it was all just as she had said. He hunted and feasted and at night he told tales of the

exploits of Fionn and the Fianna and of their lives in Ireland. Oisín had never felt as happy as he did with Niamh and before long they were married.

However, as time passed, Oisín began to think of returning home for a visit, as he had promised. Niamh didn't want him to go, but finally she agreed.

'Take my white horse,' she said. 'It will carry you safely to Ireland and back. But remember, whatever happens, you must not touch the soil of Ireland. If you do this you can never return to Tír na nÓg and you will never see me again.'

What Niamh didn't tell Oisín was that although he thought he had been away for only a few years, he had really been in Tír na nÓg for three hundred years.

Oisín set off for Ireland, but when he got there it seemed to him to be a very strange place. There was no trace of his father or the other members of the Fianna. The people he met seemed small and weak.

As he was riding through Gleann na Smól he came across some men who were trying to move a large stone that was too heavy for them.

'I will help you,' said Oisín to the men, who were terrified by this giant who had ridden up on a beautiful white horse. Stooping from his saddle, Oisín lifted the stone with one hand and hurled it across the fields. With that, the saddle girth snapped and Oisín fell from the horse.

As soon as he hit the ground, the horse disappeared. Instead of the proud young warrior the people saw an old, old man with long white hair and a white beard.

While Oisín sat on a rock recovering his senses, he remembered Niamh's final words to him as he left

Tír na nÓg: on no account was he to touch the soil of Ireland, or he would never be able to return to his beloved in the land of youth.

The people of Gleann na Smól gathered around the old man. They didn't know what to do to help him, so they brought him to a holy man who lived nearby.

'Where are my father and the Fianna?' Oisín asked in a trembling voice. When he was told that they had been dead for a long time he was heartbroken. He told tales of the many deeds of Fionn and the Fianna and their adventures together. He told the people of the time he had spent in Tír na nÓg and the beautiful wife he would never see again. He died soon afterwards, and all that was left were his beautiful stories, which will live for ever.

The Children of Lir

Once upon a time there lived a king called Lir who had four children: a daughter named Fionnuala and three sons called Aodh, Fiachra and Con. Their mother, the queen, was dead and the children missed her terribly. They missed the stories she used to tell them, the games she used to play, and the songs she sang at bedtime as she hugged them to sleep. The king saw that his children were sad and needed a mother, so he decided to marry again. His new bride was called Aoife. She was beautiful, but she was not the kind-hearted person the king thought she was.

Aoife grew jealous of the four children because their father loved them so much. She wanted the king all

to herself, so she planned to get rid of the children. She asked a druid to help her, and together they thought up a terrible spell.

In the castle grounds there was a large lake that the children loved to play beside. One day Aoife went with the children to the lakeside. As they played in the water, she suddenly pulled out a magic wand and waved it over them. There was a flash of light and the children vanished. In their place were four beautiful white swans.

One of the swans opened its beak and spoke with Fionnuala's voice:

'Oh, what have you done to us?' she asked, in a frightened voice.

'I have put a spell on you,' replied Aoife. 'Now everything you have will be mine. You will be swans for nine hundred years. You will spend the first three hundred years on this lake, the next three hundred years on the Sea of Moyle and the final three hundred years on the Isle of Glora. Only the sound of a church bell can break the spell.'

When the children did not come home that evening, the king went back to look for them by the lake. As he came near, four swans swam up to him. He was amazed when they began to call out.

'Father, Father,' they cried, 'we are your children. Aoife has placed a terrible magic spell on us.'

The king ran back to the castle and pleaded with Aoife to change the swans back into children, but she refused. Now Lir saw how selfish she was and banished her from the kingdom. He promised a reward to anyone who could break the spell, but nobody knew how to do it, for the spell was very strong.

Lir spent the rest of his life beside the lake, talking to his children, until he grew old and died. The swans were heartbroken. They no longer talked or sang, and nobody came to see them. Three hundred years passed and it was time for the swans to move to the cold and stormy Sea of Moyle between Ireland and Scotland.

The poor swans were tossed about by the wild waves and dashed against sharp rocks. It was a harsh life with little food and the years passed slowly. When the time came for them to fly to the Isle of Glora, the swans were old and tired. Although it was warmer on the island and there was lots of food, they were still very lonely. Then, one day, they heard the sound they had waited nine hundred years for. It was the sound of a church bell. The bell was ringing in the tower of a little church nearby.

An old man called Caomhóg stood outside. He was amazed to hear swans talking and listened to their sad story in astonishment. Then he went inside his church and brought out some holy water, which he sprinkled on the swans while he prayed over them. As soon as the water touched them, the swans miraculously began to change into an old, old woman and three old, old men. Lir's children were frightened. Caomhóg told them about God and his love for all people and they no longer felt scared. Fionnuala put her arms around her three brothers and all four old people fell to the ground, dead.

Caomhóg buried them in one grave. That night he dreamed he saw four swans flying up through the clouds and he knew that the children of Lir were at last on their way to Heaven to be with their mother and father again.

Deirdre of the Sorrows

King Conor Mac Nessa was attending a great feast given by his most favoured bard, Feidhlimidh Mac Dall, a man so gifted it was said that his verses could charm the birds out of the trees. All the nobles and warriors of the kingdom were there, including the Knights of the Red Branch. Even though Feidhlimidh's wife was expecting a baby, she was supervising the servants, making sure that everyone had everything they wanted.

Suddenly, the laughter and merriment were broken by a piercing scream, which sent an icy shiver down the spines of all those assembled. A sense of great sadness and misery engulfed the room. Everyone looked at Feidhlimidh's wife, who was standing stock still, mead pouring from the jug in her hand. Then she screamed a second time, an even more blood-curdling scream than the previous one, but to those watching it seemed to be coming not from her mouth, but from her unborn baby.

The king was as alarmed as everyone else and asked his chief druid, Cathbad, what this could mean.

'My king,' replied Cathbad, 'this scream from an unborn child is an evil omen. It spells danger for Ulster and is a warning that sadness will reign throughout the land. The child will be the greatest beauty ever seen in Ireland, but her beauty will tear the kingdom apart and will bring about the deaths of many men. She will be called Deirdre, and will become known as Deirdre of the Sorrows.'

A dreadful silence fell when the druid finished

speaking. He had prophesied a terrible war, the destruction of the kingdom and the end of everything the nobles and knights knew and loved.

Soon afterwards, Feidhlimidh's baby daughter was born and was named Deirdre. The Red Branch knights were afraid for their lives and they advised the king that the baby should be destroyed to save Ulster from a dreadful fate.

The king thought for a while. 'I will send Deirdre to be brought up far away, kept from the eyes of men, and I myself will marry her when she is old enough. This will prevent men fighting over her, and the kingdom will be safe.'

The knights were not happy with this, but they knew that the king had made up his mind.

Deirdre was taken away to a dense forest and

was given into the care of a wise old woman called Leabharcham. As predicted, Deirdre grew more and more beautiful with each passing year, with long golden hair and deep blue eyes. She had no one of her own age to talk to and was very lonely.

She began to have the same dream every night and told Leabharcham, 'I dream of a tall dark warrior with hair as black as a raven's wings and skin as white as snow. He is brave and fearless in battle.'

Leabharcham was very worried because she knew who the man was.

'He is Naoise, one of the three sons of Uisneach, all knights of the Red Branch. You must never mention your dream again, for you are promised to King Conor and will soon marry him.'

Deirdre begged Leabharcham to send for Naoise.

Leabarcham refused, but she felt sad that a beautiful young girl like Deirdre would have to marry the old king, and when Deirdre began to pine she gave in and arranged a meeting between the two young people. As soon as they met, Deirdre and Naoise fell in love.

'I cannot marry King Conor,' said Deirdre. 'We must go as far from Ulster as possible.'

She set out with Naoise and his brothers, travelling all around Ireland in the search for somewhere to take refuge, but everyone feared the king's anger and no one would help them. In the end, they decided that they would have to leave Ireland and set sail for a small island off the Scottish coast.

They lived there happily and peacefully for some time until, one day, a messenger arrived from the king to say that he had forgiven them and that they should come back to Ulster. Deirdre didn't trust the message but the sons of Uisneach believed it and wanted to return to Ulster. Deirdre went with them, pleading with them to turn back, but they wouldn't listen.

As soon as they landed in Ulster they were brought, not to the king's castle, but to the fort of the Red Branch knights. Deirdre was now certain that they had walked into a trap.

She was right. Soon the fort was surrounded and, although the sons of Uisneach fought bravely, they were heavily outnumbered and were quickly disarmed. The knights seized them and brought them before the king.

'Who will kill these traitors for me?' asked Conor.

None of the Red Branch knights would kill a fellow knight, but an unknown warrior from another kingdom stepped forward.

'I will kill them,' he shouted.

With a single blow of his sword the unknown warrior cut of the heads of the three sons of Uisneach. Deirdre screamed and fell to the ground beside Naoise's body. So great was her sorrow that her heart broke at that moment and she died beside him.

Feidhlimidh was so angry with the king that he left Ulster for ever and went to live in Connacht at the court of Queen Maeve. Many of Conor's warriors went with him and joined the queen's army. Later they would fight many bloody battles against the knights of the Red Branch.

In this way, the prophecy that Deirdre would bring sorrow and trouble to Ulster was fulfilled.

The Brown Bull of Cooley

Queen Maeve ruled Connacht with her husband Ailill. She was a tough ruler and both she and Ailill were very competitive. One night, they began to boast to each other about all their riches and possessions. Maeve had many beautiful jewels, but so had Ailill. Ailill had fine clothes, but so had Maeve. On and on they went, comparing their chariots, houses, lands, flocks of sheep and great herds of cattle. Anything mentioned by one of them was soon matched by the other.

Then Ailill remembered his white bull, Finnbhennach. Maeve had nothing to say to this, because none of the bulls in her herds were quite as fine as Finnbhennach.

The next day, Maeve sent for her druid.

'Tell me,' she demanded, 'where in Ireland will I find a bull as fine as Ailill's white bull, Finnbhennach?'

'The bull you are looking for is in Ulster,' replied the druid. 'It is a great brown bull that belongs to Daire Mac Fiachra, who lives in Cooley.'

Maeve sent messengers to Cooley at once, asking for a loan of the great bull for one year. In return she promised Daire Mac Fiachra a gift of 50 fine heifers. Daire was delighted with the offer and ordered a feast to be prepared for Maeve's messengers before they set off on their journey back to Connacht.

During the feast, however, one of the messengers was heard boasting that if Daire had not given the bull willingly they would have taken it by force. When this was reported back to Daire he was absolutely furious.

'Go back to Connacht and tell your queen that she will not have my bull,' he shouted, as he sent the messengers on their way.

When the messengers told Maeve that Daire had refused to lend her his bull, Maeve decided that she would capture it. She assembled a great army of all her warriors and marched to Ulster.

Now, this all happened during the winter, which was a time when the army of Ulster lay in a deep sleep, under a spell cast by the sea-witch. When Maeve's army arrived the only defenders of Ulster were Cúchulainn and the young boys training with the Red Branch. Cúchulainn knew that alone they couldn't defeat Maeve's army, but he made an agreement with her that she would send one of her heroes to fight him every day.

Day after day Cúchulainn fought Maeve's heroes, and day after day he won.

Finally, exhausted, he called on the boys of the Red Branch to defend Ulster, then he lay down and fell into a deep sleep.

Maeve took this opportunity to attack. While the battle was raging she sent some of her men to capture Daire's great brown bull.

When Cúchulainn woke up he found that the bull had gone and most of the Red Branch boys had been killed. However, spring had come and the spell of the sea-witch was broken. The men of Ulster, released from their enchantment, set off after Maeve, who was heading for Connacht, driving the bull before her.

When she arrived at her castle she ordered her men to put the bull into a pen to keep him safe. When

Ailill's bull heard the bellowing of the brown bull, he charged at the intruder. But the brown bull impaled Finnbhennach on his horns, and the white bull was killed instantly. Raging and bellowing, the brown bull broke out of its pen and thundered home to Cooley. No sooner had it reached Cooley than its heart burst and it collapsed and died.

So, in the end, despite a battle having been fought and won, neither Maeve nor Ailill was richer than the other, and no one, not even Daire, ever again possessed a fine bull that was the match of Finnbhennach or the brown bull of Cooley.

Cúchulainn

The king of Dundalk had a young son called Setanta, whose dearest wish was to become a knight of the famous Red Branch of Ulster. The king and queen had told Setanta that he could go to the special training school at the castle of his uncle Conor Mac Nessa, the king of Ulster, in Armagh, when he was old enough. He pleaded with them to be allowed to go to the Macra, as the school was known, even though he was only seven years old, but they continued to refuse.

'There is no place for a young boy like you in the rough and tumble of the court,' said his mother.

One day, Setanta decided that he couldn't wait any longer and he set off on the road to Armagh. It was a long journey, but he had brought his hurley and sliotar to play with. He would throw the sliotar as far ahead as possible, then he would run forward with his hurley to catch it before it hit the ground.

When Setanta reached King Conor's castle, he found all of the Macra boys, one hundred and fifty altogether, playing on the great plain in front of the castle. Some of them were playing hurling and he hurried over to join them in his favourite game. He scored a brilliant goal, which made the other players angry and they attacked the uninvited boy.

Setanta fought bravely, but the commotion disturbed the king, who was playing chess inside the castle. He sent a servant to see what was happening. The servant took Setanta by the arm and brought him before the king.

'Who are you?' asked the king. 'I know all the Macra boys, but I don't recognise you.'

'I am Setanta, son of your brother, the king of Dundalk. I have come here to join the Macra because I want to be a Red Branch knight as soon as I am old enough.'

The king was impressed with Setanta and agreed that he could join the Macra. Setanta settled in very quickly and enjoyed every minute of his training and education. The boys who had attacked him soon became his firm friends and everyone always wanted him to be on their team.

One day, Culann, the king's master blacksmith, who made all the spears and swords for Conor's men, invited the king and his knights to a feast. As the king's nephew, Setanta was also invited. However, when it was time to set out for the feast, Setanta was playing a game of hurling with his schoolmates and he didn't want to leave. He told the king that he would come later, when the game had finished. When the royal party arrived at Culann's home, the king forgot to tell his host that Setanta would be coming later. Time passed, the feast got under way and the king still didn't remember about Setanta. Culann unchained his wolfhound, which guarded his home at night, and released it.

The game of hurling was an exciting one and it went on for a long time. Setanta set out for the blacksmith's house as soon as it was over, but by the time he reached it night had fallen. As he approached the door he heard a ferocious and savage growling and then a large beast attacked him, jumping at him with its sharp teeth bared. Setanta was carrying no

weapons, but he hurled his sliotar down the dog's throat with all the strength he could find, then he took the animal by its hind legs and dashed it against a rock, killing it instantly.

Inside the house, the party had heard the commotion above the noise of their merry-making.

'My nephew!' cried the king. 'I had forgotten that he was to arrive later.' He rushed outside with his knights, expecting to find Setanta torn to pieces.

Imagine everyone's surprise when they discovered Setanta, alive and well, standing over the body of the dead dog.

Although Culann was very relieved that the king's nephew was safe, he was also very sad that his faithful wolfhound, who had guarded his house every night for years, had been killed. His other dogs were still puppies, so he would have no guard dog for at least a year while he trained one of the little pups and waited for it to be fully grown.

Setanta felt guilty about the dog, who had just been doing what it was trained to do.

'I will take the place of your hound until I have trained one of the puppies to be your guard dog,' he offered. Culann agreed and the king gave his permission.

From that day on Setanta was known as Cú Chulainn, which means the Hound of Culann, and he grew up to become one of the bravest knights the Red Branch had ever admitted to their ranks.

The Magic Harp

When the fierce warriors came to Ireland from the northern lands, they brought with them their own fairy people. These were known as the Tuatha Dé Danann, and their king was called the Dagda.

The Dagda had rough manners and was a ferocious warrior, but he had a lot of goodness and kindness in him as well. He had a number of wondrous possessions, among them a magic club, which was very useful in battle and a great cooking pot of plenty, which was a bottomless source of life.

However, the most amazing thing that the Dagda owned was his harp. It was made of wood from the magical oak tree encrusted with jewels and gold, and it had a limitless store of exquisite music inside it.

The harp was one of the Dagda's most precious possessions. He had simply to pluck the strings and he could make wonderful things happen. He could make the seasons change and he could make people forget their pain and sorrow. When the Tuatha Dé Danann were attacked by their enemies, the Dagda plucked the strings of his harp and all his warriors were immediately ready to go into battle, prepared to defend their people. After the battle, the Dagda was ready with his harp again with music to heal wounds and banish sorrow and misery. The healing music also made people think of better, happier times, and they celebrated their king.

The Tuatha Dé Danann's chief enemies were the Fomorians. With dark hair and eyes, they were completely different from the fair Tuatha Dé Danann.

In the middle of a battle between the two armies, the Fomorians realised that the Dagda's castle had been left unguarded. They had heard of the power of the magic harp, so they decided to steal it. They believed that if they could do that, they would defeat the Tuatha Dé Danann.

They crept into the castle and stole the harp. They knew that they had to run far, far away, so they gathered their wives and children and fled. When they had travelled a long way, they came upon a huge banqueting hall, completely abandoned.

'We'll rest for the night here,' they said. 'We've come a long way and we should be safe here.'

They sat down at the huge table, placed the harp in the centre and began to feast and celebrate.

Suddenly, the doors of the hall burst open, and there stood the Dagda and his warriors. The Fomorians jumped up, ready to defend their prize.

'Come to me,' cried the Dagda. 'Come to me, my precious harp.'

As soon as it heard its master's voice, the harp sprang from the table right into the Dagda's waiting arms. The Dagda pulled his fingers across the strings and the harp played three chords.

The harp began to hum, then everyone heard a wail so piercing and sad that the women and children were soon weeping so hard that they could no longer see. The Fomorian warriors tried to comfort their loved ones, but the music had done its magic and they could not break its power.

The warriors reached for their beautiful bronze spears, but before they could throw them, the Dagda plucked the strings of the harp again, releasing a chord that sent waves of happiness and mirth into the room. The warriors began to laugh uncontrollably, until their spears fell out of their hands and they dropped their goblets of wine. They laughed until all the strength had gone from them, and still the chord could be heard, bouncing off the walls, filling the hall and filling their ears.

The women and children were still weeping, and were astonished when they saw the laughing warriors. But before they could say anything, the Dagda touched his harp for a third time. The music that rose from it was pure and sweet, as beautiful as joy itself. This time, the harp was playing the music of sleep and no one in the hall could resist its power.

The women closed their eyes and fell asleep. The children crawled into their mothers' laps, curled up and fell into a deep sleep. The warriors could no

longer keep upright and they sat down in their chairs and fell fast asleep. Soon the music of sleep was almost drowned out by the sound of snoring.

As soon as the Dagda was sure that everyone was fast asleep, he stole away with his warriors, taking the harp with him, of course.

The Moruadh's Treasure

Donal was wandering along the beach one day when he came upon a beautiful moruadh sitting on a rock, combing her golden hair. Her red hat, without which she couldn't travel back to her home under the sea, was lying on the rock beside her. The sun was glinting off the shining iridescent scales of her tail, and Jack thought he had never in his life seen such a beautiful sight.

He invited the moruadh home for dinner and she told him stories of her life under the sea.

'Would you like to come and see my home?' she asked. 'I could come to the rocks again tomorrow and take you there.'

The next day, Donal waited at the rocks for the moruadh. When she arrived, she handed him a red hat just like hers. When he had put it on, she took his hand and they swam away together.

Down, down they went, until they came to a dry area under the water. Here was a little town, with many narrow, winding streets. The houses had roofs made of shells and all kinds of seaweed were growing in the gardens instead of trees.

The moruadh led Donal up a long, narrow street to her home. As soon as she had closed the front door, Donal could see that there were chests overflowing with gold and silver in all the rooms.

'Where on earth did you get all that treasure?' he gasped.

'Oh, it comes from the shipwrecks,' the moruadh

replied. 'Nobody needs it any more and it looks so pretty here.'

After a good dinner of fish, the moruadh brought Donal home and said she would come back to the rocks one day soon.

Donal went to the rocks every day and waited. When the moruadh didn't appear he realised that he had fallen in love with her and, it has to be said, with all her wonderful treasure. One day, just as he was about to give up, there she was, sitting on the rocks, combing her beautiful hair.

This time, Donal asked her to marry him.

'Oh, I'm not sure about that,' said the moruadh. 'I would miss my home and all my pretty things.'

'You can bring your treasures here to decorate the house,' said Donal. 'There's plenty of room and they'd

certainly brighten the place up. Why don't you bring everything here to my house?'

So the moruadh agreed to marry him. She made a few trips back to her home under the sea, bringing a large chest full of treasure each time she returned. Soon Donal's house was full of treasure and he and the moruadh were married.

At first they were very happy, but then the moruadh began to pine for her friends and her home in the little town under the sea. Donal was afraid that she'd leave him, taking all her treasure with her. He hid her red hat, because he knew that she couldn't return to the sea without it.

But the moruadh pined and pined.

'If I can't go home, I'll soon die,' she said.

Donal was worried that she'd find her hat one day and would leave him, along with all her treasure.

He moved the hat to an even safer place and he carried all the treasure into one room. He had a huge lock made for the door.

'Nobody will be able to get their hands on that,' he said to himself.

But this time the moruadh had seen where Donal had hidden her hat and, one night, when he was fast asleep, she took it and crept out of the house.

When Donal woke up and found the moruadh had gone, he knew that he would never see her again.

'Oh well,' he said, when he saw that the lock on the door of his treasure room hadn't been disturbed. 'I still have all the treasure. I'll be rich to the end of my days.'

But when he went into the room, it was completely bare. And that was the last he saw of the moruadh, or any of her kind.

Labhra's Ears

One day, a poor widow was sitting at home when the king's messenger knocked at the door.

'I have been sent by the king to bring you this message,' he said when she opened the door. 'Your son is to come to the palace tomorrow morning – the king has a very special job for him.'

The poor woman was very worried because her son was a barber, and it was well known that King Labhra summoned a barber to his palace once a year to cut his hair. It was also well known that the barbers were never seen again, although nobody knew why this should be so.

However, what nobody knew was that King Labhra

had a terrible secret. He had very strange ears, ears that were just like those of a donkey, and he had to have his hair cut in a very special way to hide them. Every barber who had cut the king's hair had been executed immediately afterwards so that he could never tell anyone the king's dreadful secret.

The barber's mother was very worried that she would never see her son again, so she went to the palace to see the king.

'My son is all that I have in the world,' she said. 'If he doesn't return to our home I will have no one to look after me.'

The king felt sorry for the old woman and thought about how he could help her.

'I will allow your son to return to you on one condition,' he said.

'Anything, anything at all,' agreed the old woman.

'Your son must promise faithfully never to tell any living person about anything he sees while he is here cutting my hair. If he makes this pledge, he will return to you on the same day.'

The old woman thought that the king's condition seemed reasonable and she agreed that her son would reveal nothing of what he saw at the palace. When she went home she swore her son to secrecy.

The next day, the barber arrived to cut the king's hair. Imagine his surprise when he saw the king's large ears poking up through his hair. However, he was a clever young man and he knew that he had to keep the secret if he wanted to survive, so he said nothing and returned home that night.

Time passed and his mother noticed that her son

wasn't very well. He couldn't sleep, he couldn't eat, and something seemed to be troubling him all the time, but whenever his mother asked him what was bothering him he refused to answer.

She decided to send for a druid, but when the druid had seen the boy he said he couldn't help him.

'He knows a terrible secret. He has promised not to tell any living person his secret, but unless he tells someone he won't get better.'

The druid thought about the problem for a long time. Then he said, 'I have a solution. Your son must go into the forest until he reaches the tall willow tree that grows beside the stream. If he whispers his secret to the leaves he will be cured, and the promise will not be broken because he will not have told a living person.'

The boy followed the advice of the druid, travelling deep into the forest until he found the tree.

'King Labhra has donkey's ears,' he whispered to the tree as the leaves rustled in the wind. Immediately he felt a heavy weight lift from his shoulders and from that day his health improved.

However, a few months later the king's harpist dropped his harp during a banquet and he went into the forest to find some wood for a new one. When he found a large willow beside the stream he decided that it would be perfect. He took his axe and began to chop down the tree. He chose the wood he needed and went home to make a new harp.

When the harp was finished, the harpist was called before the king to entertain his chieftains. As he began to pluck the strings of his new harp, a strange music filled the hall.

'The king, the king has donkey's ears, has donkey's ears,' sang a reedy voice.

The king gasped when he realised that his dreadful secret had been revealed, terrified that he would be laughed at. However, when he saw that no one was laughing at him he knew that he would never have to hide his donkey's ears again.

From that day forward the king was proud of his unusual ears . . . and all the barbers in the kingdom were safe.

Paddy and the Pooka

Paddy loved stories about pookas, who were well known for playing jokes on people. They could be fierce and frightening, or kind and helpful, and could speak as if they were human. He listened intently to his grandmother tell tales of the pookas and knew that they appeared in different guises. Their favourite was that of a sleek black horse, but they could also appear as little goblins or other creatures.

One day, Paddy was outside tending the cattle, when he felt an odd wind – it must be a pooka, going to where the fairies danced!

'Pooka!' he called out. 'Let me see you!' Suddenly, a bull charged at Paddy! He quickly threw his coat on the bull, which stopped in its tracks and said, 'Go to

the mill tonight when the moon is full and you'll have good luck!'

Paddy knew at once that the bull was a pooka and decided to do as he had been told. He was very excited and hoped that the pooka would bring good fortune.

That night, Paddy went to the mill. There were sacks of corn lying around waiting to be ground into flour, but the men who worked there were fast asleep. Paddy was tired and went to sleep too. When he woke up, the corn had all been ground into flour, even though all the men were still sleeping soundly. For several nights the same thing happened. Paddy decided he would have to stay awake and see how the corn was ground! He crept into an old chest in a corner and pulled the lid down. The chest had a big keyhole and he could peep out and see what was going on.

Paddy waited until it was very late. At exactly midnight, he spied six little fairy men, each carrying a sack of corn. They were followed by an old man in ragged clothes. Paddy couldn't believe his eyes! He peeped through the keyhole and tried to keep as quiet as he could so that he wouldn't be found. The little people set to work, and soon all the corn was ground. Paddy knew the old man was the pooka he had met a few days before.

In the morning, Paddy told his father what he had seen. His father came with him that night and hid in the old chest with Paddy. Sure enough, the six little men and the ragged old pooka appeared at midnight to grind the corn. In the morning, all the sacks of flour were ready for market.

'I shall let the pookas do their good work,' his

father said, 'but I will sack my lazy men.' Paddy's father did as he said and soon became very rich, but he never spoke of the pooka, for that was known to bring bad luck.

Paddy often hid in the chest to watch the pooka. He was sad that the old man, who worked so hard, had only tattered rags to wear. So he saved up his pocket money until he had enough to buy a splendid suit of clothes, which would keep the pooka warm in the cold mill. One night, before climbing into the chest, he laid the clothes out on the floor. When the old pooka came in, he was amazed.

'Fine clothes for me?' he cried. 'I shall be a well-dressed gentleman.'

The pooka put the suit on and paraded about. He looked at the corn, waiting to be ground. 'No more work for me!' he cried. 'I'm a gentleman now, too grand to grind corn!'

He kicked his old rags into the corner and disappeared into the darkness. No corn was ground ever again by the pooka.

But by now, Paddy's father was very rich. He had no men to pay and had more flour to sell than he had ever had before. He was so rich that he sold his mill and bought a fine house with stables and servants. Paddy was brought up to be a gentleman and sent away to school. When he returned, he married a woman who was so beautiful that all the people of the village thought that she must be a daughter of the king of the fairies.

Something very odd happened at their wedding. When all the guests stood up to drink to their health, a golden cup of wine appeared in the middle of the table, as if by magic.

Paddy knew at once that it was a gift from the pooka. He and his beautiful bride drank from the golden cup. They lived happily ever after and led prosperous lives. The golden cup was their most treasured possession and it was passed down to their children and their descendants. It is still in their possession to this day.

Granuaile

The great chieftain Eoghan Dubh Dara had a daughter who had been christened Gráinne. She grew up in Belclare Castle, a fortified tower with a great hall where the clans would gather for huge feasts. From a very young age, Gráinne had loved to go with her father on board one of his large fleet of ships. Because she was a girl, Eoghan did his best to discourage her, but she was determined to have a more exciting life than could be expected by a girl in those times.

One day, Gráinne cut off all her hair, borrowed her brother's clothes and demanded to be taken on her father's next voyage. Her father ignored her mother's anger and agreed that she could go with him. This was the beginning of Gráinne's life on the high seas. Because she had cut off her hair she was known as Gráinne Mhaol (Bald Grace) or Granuaile.

When she was of marriageable age, a match was arranged for her with the leader of the O'Flaherty clan. He was an acclaimed fighter, known as Donal an Chogaidh (Donal of the Battles). Her parents had hoped that he would tame their wild daughter, but instead she became involved in the battles of her husband's clan. Her father had taught her how to use weapons and her skill impressed everyone. When Donal was killed in an ambush, Granuaile defended his castle against their enemies.

Although the O'Flaherty clan admired Granuaile, they would not accept her leadership after he was killed, so she returned to her parents' home. Eoghan was very proud of his daughter's exploits and he gave her his castle on Clare Island. She set herself up as chieftain there, with two hundred followers. With her experience of the seafaring life she decided to become a pirate, and became renowned as the most daring and feared pirate on the west coast of Ireland. Her treasure chests were soon overflowing.

The English realised that Granuaile would have to be stopped. They sent a naval force after her under the command of Sir Richard Bingham, the governor of Connacht. He captured her and threatened to execute her for piracy, but imprisoned her instead, together with her brother and her son. She spent two years in Dublin Castle, an imprisonment that almost broke her health and her spirit. She was released when she promised that she would give up her life of piracy. However, her brother and son remained imprisoned.

By this time, Granuaile was growing old and she decided to seek the protection of the English queen, Elizabeth. She wrote to her and Elizabeth asked her to come to London to meet her.

Granuaile's clothing was that of an Irish clan leader and was coarse and rough compared to the finery of the English court. Her velvet cloak was old and worn and pinned to her shoulder with a gold brooch, her only sign of wealth. Her hair was wild and undressed and the courtiers looked down their noses at her.

'Do not sneer at me, you popinjays!' she roared. 'Do not believe that I am not an important person because I do not wear fine clothes like your queen. In my own lands I am as powerful and important as your gracious queen.' She brushed the courtiers aside and strode off to meet the queen in her presence chamber.

The two women looked each other in the eye. They each knew that the other was brave and fearless.

'You are most welcome to my court,' said the queen. 'Please sit by my side and let us talk.'

Granuaile bowed her head and sat beside the queen. They made a strange pair, both proud, both no longer young. There the similarity ended. Granuaile was dressed plainly and unfashionably, while the queen was beautifully dressed in the latest fashion and wearing a whole treasury of jewels.

The two women spoke for a long time, to the amazement of all the courtiers. When Granuaile walked out of the court that day, she held her head even higher than when she had arrived. Elizabeth had granted every one of her requests. Her brother and son were released from prison, and she was given a pension for the rest of her life.

Granuaile lived into her seventies, an old age for the time. Even when she was an old woman she remained a leader, admired by all her followers. By a strange coincidence she died in 1603, the same year as Queen Elizabeth, another fearless woman who had defied convention and who, despite their very different lives, had understood Granuaile better than most.

Brian Boru

After long years of invasion the Vikings had gradually imposed their rule in Ireland. The people were unhappy with this occupation and rebelled against it continually. Brian, the young son of Cennetig, the king of Munster, and a warrior from the tribe of Dál Cais, had been in the saddle for many hours, fighting a long battle. He was utterly weary but he refused to show it, such was his determination to win the battle and defeat the Vikings once and for all.

Brian's older brother, Mahon, had succeeded his father as king of Munster and Brian had no claim to the throne. However, Brian had a secret: he had been told by a fortune teller that he would one day be king, not just of Munster, but of all Ireland.

As Brian looked around the battlefield, he saw the Vikings preparing to charge. He gripped his spear and looked around for Mahon, who was in the thick of the fighting. This time, the Vikings were too strong to withstand, and the Dál Cais warriors were forced back to the gates of their fort. Brian watched in horror as the Viking horde ran through the settlement, killing, burning and plundering.

The next day, the whole settlement lay under a pall of smoke. Brian and Mahon's mother had been killed in the raid, along with many of the other inhabitants of the settlement.

'I pledge today that I will avenge the death of our mother and will not rest until these Norsemen have been driven from Ireland for ever!' Brian swore to his older brother.

Mahon saw the cold rage in Brian's eyes and realised that although he was still young in years, his brother was no longer a boy.

'Bravely spoken, my brother!' he cried. 'We will fight side by side and I will be proud to have you with me.'

The years passed and there were many more fierce battles. Brian grew taller, stronger and braver.

Then, one day, Mahon called him to his side and said that he thought he should propose a treaty with the Vikings. 'They are too strong for us,' he said. 'We cannot allow this bloodshed to continue.'

But Brian remembered how the Vikings had killed their mother and he knew that he could never bow to them. He broke with his brother and waited for his chance to fight. Many warriors came with him, for he was skilled in warfare and tactics and was renowned for his bravery.

Finally, Brian got his chance to fight the Vikings at a great battle in Munster between the Dál Cais and a huge army led by Imar, the Viking ruler of Limerick. Imar's army routed the Dál Cais and Mahon was killed, which meant that Brian was now king of Munster. Imar's success was short-lived, for Brian challenged him to a fight and killed him.

As ruler of Munster he joined forces with the rulers of Connacht and Leinster, and they divided the country between them. Brian defeated the Vikings once again at the Battle of Gleann Máma and demanded the kingship of all Ireland. In 1002, Brian was declared high king of Ireland. He collected tributes from the minor kings, which he used to rebuild the monasteries and libraries destroyed during the Viking invasions and became known as Brian Bóruma, Brian of the Tributes.

Brian wanted to restore peace and prosperity to the land. He ruled his warriors with a firm hand so that farmers could return to their land and teachers to their classrooms. He travelled around the country with a grand entourage so that the people could see him and pay homage. Under his rule there was peace in the land for many years.

However, there were those who thought Brian ruled with too strong a hand and some of the people became resentful of his power. The Viking king of Leinster decided to challenge the high king and gathered together a huge army.

The opposing armies met at Clontarf on 23 April 1014 for the fiercest battle in the history of Ireland.

They fought all day and the Vikings were finally driven into the sea. While Brian was offering prayers of thanks for his victory a small band of Viking warriors crept up on him and killed him. Within hours of winning the greatest battle of his long reign, Brian lay dead on the battlefield.

His heartbroken warriors waked him for 12 days and 12 nights. Bards sang of his exploits and storytellers told tales of his courageous deeds. His body was then taken in great state to Armagh where he was finally laid to rest.

Brain Boru is renowned as the greatest warrior Ireland has ever known.

Saint Brendan and the Whale

When Saint Brendan was almost 85 years old, with white hair and an aching back, he decided to travel in a simple coracle from Ireland to the 'Promised Land of the Saints'. Nobody knew if it really existed, but Brendan was absolutely determined to find it.

It was a very brave decision for an old man to make. Most of his fellow monks thought he was completely mad, and told him so when he joined them in the monastery for what would be his last meal on dry land for a very long time indeed!

The following morning dawned bright and cold, which made Brendan happy, for these were ideal sailing conditions. He had a simple breakfast of porridge, then he walked to the shore with his crew. After the abbot had blessed the monks and the seemingly outlandish venture they were embarking on, the little crew climbed into the coracle, Brendan smiling confidently as he took his place in the small craft.

As they sailed away, he watched the coastline of Ireland growing smaller and smaller. At last, all he could see around him was the great empty sea. For many days the monks had no sight of land, and their food and water supplies were running very low. They managed to catch some fish, but they were very relieved when they saw land in the far distance. As they came closer, they realised that it was an island, home to hundreds of sheep. Brendan was keeping a diary of their voyage and when he wrote his usual report that night he called the place the Isle of Sheep, or the Faroe Islands.

The next morning, Brendan decided that they should light a fire and celebrate Mass. They came to a hill by the shore overlooking the island and the surrounding sea, and Brendan asked the younger monks to build a fire there. As it burned away merrily, Brendan prepared for Mass.

Suddenly the ground began to shake beneath their feet and the monks looked around in terror. What on earth was happening? Was it an earthquake? Horrified, they watched as the fire slid down the moving hill towards the sea, and they had to jump out of its path as it approached them. Brendan was amazed to see a large eye appearing out of the hill. A deep voice asked, 'Who is setting fire to my back?'

At that, the terrified monks ran away, all except Brendan, who stood his ground.

'Who are you and where are you?' he asked.

The great eye blinked slowly and turned in his direction as the ground started to heave again. Brendan was knocked to his knees as the hill moved upwards. Now he could see that what he was kneeling on was no hill – it was a huge whale!

'My name is Jasconius. As you can see, I am a whale,' said the deep voice.

And that was the truth. The monks had climbed a great whale who had been sleeping peacefully by the shore, half in and half out of the water. Brendan tried to pour water over the whale's back where the monks had lit their fire, but he felt the whale's body shaking and stopped. Then he realised that the creature was laughing at him.

'Don't worry,' said the whale. 'Your fire has woken

me up, but it didn't hurt me at all. I have extremely thick skin.'

Meanwhile, the monks were feeling ashamed of their cowardice and crept back to see what had happened to Brendan. Imagine their surprise when they found him sitting in the sand, talking to a mighty whale.

'My friends, there is no reason to be frightened,' Brendan called to them. 'This noble creature has offered to send messages to all the whales so that we can travel safely between here and the Promised Land.'

And Jasconius was as good as his word. For the remainder of their voyage, whenever Brendan and his monks met any whales, the creatures would leap and play around their little boat, but they did them no harm and pointed out the safest passage for the next stage of the journey.

Finally, the little band of monks arrived at a beautiful island, which, Brendan felt sure, was the 'Promised Land of the Saints'. Although he was weary from his travels, his heart almost burst with joy.

'Brothers, we have reached our destination! This is the Promised Land! Give thanks to God!' He then led the monks in prayers of thanksgiving and joyful singing.

The long journey had taken seven years. Some people believe that the Promised Land was America, although it would be another nine hundred years before another man made a similar voyage. That man's name was Christopher Columbus.

Saint Patrick and the Shamrock

Patrick sat on the hard bench of a small boat as it rolled with the swell of the sea. Peering into the mist, he could just about make out the shoreline. He was returning to Ireland, a place he had been sent to as a slave when he was just 16 years old. Put to work in the hills as a swineherd, he had eventually escaped to France, where he became a priest. It was there that he had a dream, telling him to take God's message to the people of Ireland.

Patrick watched as the boatmen skilfully guided the little craft in between the jagged rocks close to the shore, then he heard the scraping of stones against the bottom of the boat. Pulling his rough woollen robes up around his waist, he jumped into the water and began to wade ashore. The sailors shouted their farewells and turned the little boat around to head out to sea again.

Patrick stood on the beach, watching the boat disappear over the horizon. His mission to convert the pagan people of Ireland to Christianity was about to begin.

Soon after he arrived in Ireland, Patrick heard that Laoghaire, the high king, had summoned all the chieftains of Ireland to a feast at Tara. The druids were going to celebrate the coming of spring with a special ceremony. Laoghaire ordered all the lights and fires in the surrounding countryside to be put out until a great fire was lit on the royal Hill of Tara.

The pagan festival took place at the same time as the Christian feast of Easter. Patrick decided to use the opportunity to show the pagan people the power of Christianity. He went with his followers to the Hill of Slane, across the valley from the Hill of Tara, and they lit a huge fire there that blazed into the night sky.

The druids were very angry when they saw this. They believed that Patrick wanted to be stronger than the high king and they told Laoghaire that he must defeat Patrick if he was to keep his power over the people. They lit their fire on the Hill of Tara and soon the whole valley was lit up by the huge fires that were blazing at either end. It was a spectacular sight and people talked about it for many years to come.

The king marched with his soldiers and the druids across the valley to Slane. They tried in vain to put out Patrick's fire, but it continued to burn. They tried to kill Patrick, but he stood bravely in front of the fire, singing hymns and giving praise to God. The fire burned throughout the night and its light shone across the land. The king realised that Patrick could not be defeated by force and he began to think that the druids might not have all the answers after all. The next day, Laoghaire sent an invitation to Patrick to come to Tara and tell him about Christianity.

On the road to Tara, Patrick saw some shamrock, a plant that was sacred to the druids, growing by the roadside and he stooped down to pick a bunch; he tucked it away in his robes and continued on his way.

When Patrick arrived at Tara, the king listened to everything he had to say about God and the Gospels and Christian belief. Some of it was very difficult to understand, especially the idea of the Trinity: how could God actually be three people – the Father, the Son and the Holy Spirit?

Suddenly, Patrick remembered the shamrock he had picked and he had an idea. He pulled the bunch out of his robes and broke off a single stem. There were three leaves on the one stem, three in one – just like the Trinity.

That day, the king came to understand Christianity and realised that Patrick was not in competition with him and didn't want to be more powerful than him. He gave him permission to preach the Gospel throughout the land.

Patrick spent the rest of his days travelling the length and breadth of Ireland, spreading the word of God and establishing the Christian faith throughout the land. Eventually, he became the patron saint of

Ireland and his feast day is celebrated every year on 17 March, not just in Ireland, but around the world.

And that is how the shamrock came to be the emblem of Ireland.

Saint Patrick Banishes the Snakes

Long, long ago in Ireland, snakes were a big problem. People were always finding them where they weren't wanted – hiding in their drains, snuggling up in their hay barns and lurking under the cabbage leaves in the vegetable patch, and sometimes they would even find one curled up in the fireplace during the summer.

Everyone was fed up with the snakes – they frightened their children and made it very difficult for people to harvest their beans and wheat. You never knew what you might find lurking in the fields and among the vines!

Finally, the people decided they had had enough. They had heard that Patrick had amazing powers and they sent a delegation to him to ask if he could do anything for them.

Saint Patrick had never seen so many snakes anywhere as he had in Ireland, so he agreed that there was a big problem. He thought and thought about what he could do, and then he hit on a great idea. He told the delegation to go home and tell everyone not to worry, he would soon get rid of the snakes for them.

Patrick knew that snakes were frightened of vibration, so he rooted around in his belongings for his big drum. He strapped it to his chest and set out for a cliff at the edge of the sea. As he walked he banged the drum in a loud, steady beat. Soon, a lot of people had come out of their houses, wondering what all the rumpus was about. They began to follow Patrick.

When they had all gathered on the cliff, they could see that they were being followed by hundreds and hundreds of snakes, driven out of their hiding places by the vibration of Patrick's drum. The crowd started cheering, because they could see that the snakes were heading straight for the sea!

Then disaster struck – the drum broke. Everyone held their breath, wondering if the snakes would just turn back and return to their hiding places. A huge snake slithered back down the hill, laughing at Patrick because he thought he was powerless without his drum.

Then, an amazing thing happened. An angel appeared out of heaven and quickly mended the drum. Patrick started to beat the drum again and soon the last snake had slithered, as fast as it could, into the sea.

Everyone was delighted to get rid of the snakes at last, and they had a huge celebration, which went on for several days and nights.

However, as soon as Patrick returned home after the party, he was greeted by the old serpent who lived in the lake beside his home.

'You don't get rid of me that easily,' said the wily serpent. 'As soon as I laid eyes on that drum of yours, I knew what you were about, so I hid under a big stone on the bed of the lake. Catch me if you can,' it hissed, as it slid back into the lake.

Patrick knew that his drum was powerless against this snake, so he began to make a small wooden box. He set up his workbench outside, right beside the lake. The serpent soon came slithering out of the lake to see what was going on.

'What are you making?' he asked.

'It's a box for you,' replied the saint, without looking up from his task.

'Don't be ridiculous,' replied the serpent. 'I'd never fit in that. It's far too small.'

'Nonsense,' said Patrick, 'I made it specially and it's just the right size for you. Why don't you try it and see?'

'Oh, very well, then,' grumbled the snake. 'I love proving you wrong.'

And with that, he crawled into the box and Patrick snapped the lid shut. He brought the box to the cliff and threw it into the sea.

And that was the end of the last snake that ever lived in Ireland.

A Prince in Disguise

The Fianna had camped overnight on the Hill of Howth and were now preparing themselves for a long day's hunting.

'This will be a good day,' said Conán Maol. 'I feel very well so I will run fast. I know that I will run faster than anyone else today.'

The other members of the Fianna laughed at this, because Conán was short and fat and not built for running. Suddenly, they heard a voice coming from a nearby bush.

'Fast? You think you can run fast? Rubbish! No one can outrun me, especially not you!'

The Fianna looked around for whoever had made

this outrageous statement, but they could see no one. Then, out from the bush stepped a strange-looking old man with a long, white beard. He was wearing a long, tattered and patched coat that reached right down to the ground. His boots were enormous and so caked with mud that it was hard to see how he could lift his feet to walk, let alone run.

The Fianna were giving all their attention to the strange old man and nobody had noticed a large ship sailing into Dublin Bay. Nor had they noticed the tall warrior who had jumped ashore and was now striding across the beach towards them, his golden helmet glinting in the sun and his purple cloak blowing out behind him. He was the very picture of a strong, brave warrior.

The Fianna were taken by surprise, but they gathered their wits quickly and their leader, Fionn, stepped forward.

'Welcome,' he said to the stranger. But before he could say anything else, the warrior stretched out his arm and pointed to the Fianna.

'I offer a challenge,' he declared. 'Choose your swiftest runner to race against me. The winner will have as a prize all the gold, all the horses and all the chariots of Éire.'

'Caoilte Mac Rónáin is our fastest runner,' said Fionn, 'but he is away in Tara, so we would like to postpone the race.'

'No!' said the warrior. 'The race must take place now. That is my challenge.'

The Fianna were worried, because they knew that none of those present could beat the warrior in a race. Then the old man stepped forward.

'In that case,' he said, 'I will accept your challenge.

What distance did you have in mind?'

'I never race fewer than 60 miles,' replied the warrior.

'Fine,' said the old man calmly. 'If Fionn will lend us two horses, we can ride that distance today and race back tomorrow.'

Fionn agreed to lend a horse to the warrior and another to the old man. The Fianna were stunned. They could not understand how Fionn was allowing this to happen. This old man couldn't win the race for them!

The Fianna rode with the warrior and the old man for 60 miles, then they pitched camp. The warrior retired early, but the old man stayed up late with the Fianna, singing and carousing.

The next morning the warrior was up and about

early, anxious to begin the race. He went to the old man's tent to wake him.

'I wouldn't dream of running so early in the morning,' said the old man. 'But if you're in such a rush, off you go and I'll follow you later.' The warrior immediately set off while the old man curled up and fell fast asleep again.

When he woke again it was mid-morning, so he decided to leave without having any breakfast.

He was a sight to behold as he followed the route taken by the warrior, the tails of his long coat flapping in the wind behind him as he jumped and hopped along the road. He never broke into a run but, even so, it wasn't long before he had caught up with the warrior.

'We're halfway there now,' he said to the warrior.

'Have you stopped for something to eat yet?'

The warrior didn't reply, so the old man went ahead, stopping when he saw some blackberry bushes, heavy with ripe fruit.

'Well, I'm hungry, so I'm going to stop and have something to eat,' he muttered to himself. He began to gobble up the blackberries, and by the time the warrior had caught up with him his coat and face were stained with purple juice.

'Your coat tails are caught up in a bush ten miles back,' snarled the warrior as he passed him at top speed.

'I knew I'd lost something,' said the old man. 'I'd better go back to get them.' He ran backwards, retrieved his coat tails and in three long hops he had caught up with the warrior again.

Meanwhile, Fionn and the Fianna had ridden back to the Hill of Howth and were watching out for the runners.

'Do you see anything?' asked Fionn.

'I can see something in the far distance,' said Conán Maol.

When the runners approached, the Fianna gave a great cheer of joy and relief when they saw the old man well in the lead. But then they heard a fearsome roar and saw the warrior approaching the old man, sword drawn. He swung it at the old man, but the next thing the Fianna saw was the warrior's head rolling along beside the old man. How on earth had the old man managed to do that?

'Let that be a lesson to you,' said the old man. 'It's lucky for you that I'm feeling generous today.' And he

reached down, picked up the head and threw it onto the warrior's shoulders, where it landed back to front!

The warrior ran backwards to his ship and sailed away as fast as he could.

While all this was happening, Fionn had realised who the old man was.

'Thank you, thank you,' he said, 'for saving the honour of the Fianna and making us rich. I know now that you are the prince from Tír na nÓg who becomes human once a year.'

'I have enjoyed my time here,' said the old man, 'but now I must return to my people.' He hopped off into the distance and, just as he turned to wave goodbye, he changed into a tall, fair-haired prince.

As the Fianna watched, a white mist descended on him and by the time it had cleared he had disappeared, leaving them alone on the Hill of Howth again.

The Magic Cloak

Eoin was hiding behind a rock, watching the tide ebb far out into the bay. He had been waiting years for this day to come. He had been listening to the tales of the old people in his village since he was a very young boy and he knew that on a particular day every seven years something very strange happened.

The old people said that once every seven years the sea went out as far as the horizon and it was then that the fairy people appeared. The fairies spread a magic cloak in the centre of the sands and this had the power to hold back the tide. Whoever owned the cloak could order the sea to stay back and could farm the dry land, which was very fertile.

Eoin really needed some good land to farm and he had always listened very carefully to this story. Seven years ago he had crept out and watched from behind a rock as the waves rolled back and the fairy people appeared. This time he had brought his horse and had tethered it nearby.

The fairy people arrived at dawn. Eoin could barely make out their shapes through the sea mist, but he could hear the lilting music of their fiddles and harps.

He mounted his horse very quietly, making sure not to startle the animal. Just then, the mist lifted, and Eoin saw the strangest sight. The sea and sand had completely disappeared and in their place there was a green plain as far as he could see.

Eoin knew that if he could get his hands on the magic cloak the land would be his! But the cloak was guarded by leprechauns and he could see them sitting on it in a circle, repairing piles of tiny shoes, tapping in the nails in time to the music.

The edges of the cloak were flapping in the breeze. Eoin thought that if he could grab the edge, he could pull the cloak from under the leprechauns. He pulled gently on the reins of his horse and moved forward. However, it was taking much longer than he had expected to reach the cloak. Whenever he looked back the shoreline seemed to be very far away.

When he finally reached the part of the shoreline where the leprechauns were sitting he slowed his horse and dismounted a short distance away from them. He crept forward, and was sure that they must be able to hear his heart thumping or the sound of his breathing. But the leprechauns continued to work.

As soon as he was close enough, Eoin reached out and took hold of a corner of the cloak. Grasping it firmly, he gave a sudden tug and pulled it from under the leprechauns. He threw the cloak on his back, mounted his horse and galloped towards the shore. He could hear all kinds of chaos and confusion behind him but he didn't dare look back.

Suddenly it got quiet, very, very quiet. The wind dropped and an eerie calm descended.

'I've made it!' Eoin thought triumphantly.

Then he heard a rumbling noise, getting louder and louder every second. He looked over his shoulder and there, racing towards him, as fast as a train, was a gigantic wave! The fairy wave raced towards him as he urged his mount on. Suddenly, he was swept off the horse. He felt as if he was being pulled in several directions at once and being beaten by many pairs of little hands.

Then the wave disappeared as quickly as it had appeared and Eoin fell into a deep sleep. When he woke up, every bone and muscle in his body was aching.

'I've survived the fairy wave,' he thought, feeling behind him for the cloak on his back. 'I have the magic cloak. I can control the sea and I'll soon be rich. I have beaten the fairies, so it's worth the pain.'

His hand finally found the cloak, but instead of the magic fabric, all he could feel was a thick layer of slimy seaweed.

And that was the last time the leprechauns allowed anyone to steal the cloak. To this day, if you go down to the shore every seven years on the anniversary of Eoin's adventure, you'll see the leprechauns sitting on a cloak, laughing and singing as they repair their tiny shoes.

Soul Cages

One day, Jack was out walking on the beach when he met a moruadh, sitting on the rocks at the end of the beach near Jack's house. Jack crossed the rocks slowly and carefully – he had never met a sea fairy and he didn't want to frighten it away.

'Good day to you, Jack,' said the moruadh.

'How do you know my name?' asked Jack, astonished.

'Your grandfather was a great friend of mine,' the moruadh said. 'We often used to enjoy a drink together, so of course I know who you are.'

'Where do you find something to drink under the sea?' asked Jack. 'I thought it was all salt water.'

178

'Ah well,' said the moruadh, 'there are barrels and bottles in the ships that sink. Why don't you meet me here tomorrow and I'll take you to my house so that you can try some.'

Jack was very surprised, but he thought that if the moruadh had been a friend of his grandfather's it would be all right to go with him to his home.

The next day, Jack went out to the rocks again. The moruadh was there, holding two red hats.

'I've borrowed a hat for you,' he said. 'As long as you're wearing it you'll be able to breathe under water. Put it on, jump in and hold on to my tail.'

The moruadh put on his own hat and jumped into the sea. Jack put on the hat the moruadh had given him, then jumped into the sea and caught hold of the moruadh's tail. Down they swam through the water until they reached a flat, dry sandy area. There were fish swimming overhead and seaweed rose up like trees. They stopped at a little cottage, which had smoke coming out of the chimney. Jack found it hard to believe that he was really under the sea!

Inside the cottage they had a splendid meal of fish, washed down with delicious liquids from the moruadh's enormous collection of bottles. The moruadh told Jack his name was Coomara.

There were rows of wicker cages, a little like lobster pots, stacked up against one wall of the cottage.

'What do you keep in those?' he asked Coomara.

'Oh, those are the soul cages,' Coomara replied. 'I put them out whenever there's a storm. The souls of drowned fishermen and sailors creep into them, then I bring them back here to keep them warm and dry.'

Jack peered closely into a couple of cages near where he was standing. He couldn't see anything, but he could hear the sound of wailing and crying. He felt very sorry for the souls, shut up in cages when they should be on their way to Heaven. What could he do to help them? He would have to think about that, but he was determined to come up with a solution.

When the time came for him to go home, Jack thanked Coomara for his great evening, then he took hold of the moruadh's tail and they swam to the beach near Jack's house. They arranged to meet again the next day, then Coomara turned around and waved as he disappeared into the sea again.

Sitting at home, Jack thought hard about what he could do for the poor trapped souls. At last he worked out a plan. When he met Coomara the next day he invited him to his house. Like the moruadh,

Jack collected bottles washed up on shore after storms and shipwrecks and he had a great collection of fine brandies.

That evening, Jack stoked up the fire so the house was nice and warm, and when Coomara arrived he sat him down beside the fire and produced some of the brandy. Coomara drank a glass or two, while Jack sipped at his very slowly. Soon the old moruadh had fallen asleep by the fire.

Jack took Coomara's red hat off his head very carefully so as not to disturb the snoring moruadh. He ran to the rocks, jammed the hat on his head and jumped into the sea. He remembered how to find Coomara's house and as soon as he got there he collected all the soul cages and brought them outside. He opened each cage and shook it. Every time he did that, there was a tiny flicker of light from the cage and he could hear a faint whistle. When every cage had been opened, Jack shut them again and put them back against the wall where he'd found them. Then he went home, where he found Coomara still fast asleep by the fire and he replaced the red hat on his head.

When he woke up, the moruadh thanked Jack and left. Jack was worried about what Coomara would say when he discovered that his soul cages were empty, but he never even noticed!

Jack and Coomara remained friends, and whenever there had been a storm he'd invite Coomara over and bring out his collection of brandy, then he'd borrow his red hat and slip down to rescue any souls trapped in the cages.

A Stranger's Gold

One beautiful day in May, Bill Doody was sitting on a rock beside a tranquil lake in Killarney. He should have been enjoying the view over the sunlit water, but instead he was staring into the distance without seeing anything. He was thinking about his wife and children and what the future held for them.

'The rent is due again tomorrow and I haven't any money to pay it,' he said to himself. 'What on earth are we going to do?' he despaired. 'If I can't pay the rent, everything we own will be confiscated and we'll all be thrown out of the house to starve at the side of the road.'

He thought he was completely alone, so he got quite a fright when a tall, well-built man suddenly appeared from behind a clump of gorse growing by the lakeside.

'What's the matter with you?' the stranger asked Bill. 'You have a very long face, as if the troubles of the world were weighing you down.'

Bill wondered who the man could be and where he could have come from. He had a strange, other-worldly air, as if he didn't really belong beside this lake in Killarney. However, he decided that no harm could come from answering the stranger.

'My cows have stopped giving milk, so I have no butter to sell for money to pay the rent with, and if I don't pay it by midday tomorrow, I will be turned off my farm. I have a wife and little children, and I don't know what will become of us all if that happens. I really don't know what to do.'

'That's a very sad tale,' said the stranger. 'But if you

tell your landlord how hard things are for you at the moment, surely he wouldn't be so cruel as to turn you out of your home?'

'You don't know my landlord,' said Bill. 'He's a very hard man, and he's had his eye on my farm for some time. He wants to give it to one of his relatives, so he's looking for any excuse to get rid of us. I'll get no help from him.'

Bill's hat was lying on the ground beside him. When he had finished telling his tale, he was about to get up and leave, but the stranger pulled a fat purse out of his pocket, opened the strings and began to pour gold coins in a steady stream into Bill's hat.

'Take this gold,' he said to Bill. 'Use it to pay your rent tomorrow and ask for a receipt. You'll soon find out that the gold won't do your landlord any good. I remember better times, when I would have dealt very severely with such a greedy, unkind man.'

Bill stared at the gold in amazement. When he turned to thank the stranger, he had disappeared. Then Bill saw him, far away in the distance, riding a beautiful white horse across the surface of the lake. He thought he must be dreaming so he rubbed his eyes, but he could still see the rider. Suddenly he realised who the stranger was.

'It was O'Donoghue!' he shouted. 'It was the great O'Donoghue!' Bill had been brought up on stories about the ancient prince, a wise and just ruler who had gone to live in a palace in Tír na nÓg. Sometimes he returned to help lost travellers and poor people.

Bill raced home to tell his wife the good news and

show her the gold. She couldn't believe how their luck seemed to be changing.

'The one thing I don't understand,' said Bill to his wife, 'is why the prince said the gold wouldn't do our landlord any good.' Puzzled, they both went to bed.

The next day, Bill was up bright and early and he went straight over to his landlord's house.

'Hand over your rent,' the landlord snarled. 'If it's a penny short, you'll be out on your ear by nightfall.'

'Here's your rent,' said Bill. 'Please count it and then give me a receipt.'

The landlord was expecting to see piles of copper coins, perhaps a few silver ones, or a grubby banknote or two. When he saw the gold coins he was stunned. He counted them quickly – it was the exact amount Bill owed for his rent. The landlord bit into some of the coins to see if they were genuine and he almost broke his teeth on them.

Instead of being happy that Bill had paid on time and in full, he was absolutely furious, because he really wanted to get his hands on Bill's farm to give to his relatives. Speechless with anger, he wrote out a receipt for the rent and pushed it across his desk into Bill's hand. Then he got up from behind the desk and showed Bill to the door. When he returned to his desk, instead of a pile of gold coins, he saw a pile of little gingerbread cakes, each with the king's head stamped on it, just like a coin. He raged and swore, but he had given Bill a receipt for his rent, so there was nothing he could do, except eat the gingerbread, which he did. It stuck in his throat, but he ate it all, because he knew that if anyone ever found out how Bill had got the better of him he'd be a laughing stock for ever.

The Crock of Gold

One clear, moonlit night, Cormac was walking home from the village. Suddenly, he heard a very peculiar noise coming from the bushes just ahead. His mother had told him that the fairy people appeared at night and had warned him to ignore any strange sounds that he heard after dark. Despite this, Cormac paused for a moment, then curiosity overcame him and he moved closer to the bushes to find out where the noise was coming from.

Imagine his surprise when he saw a little man, no bigger than his hand, trying to disentangle his beard from the bush where it had been caught as he passed by. He was wearing brown trousers and a green waistcoat and had a bright red hat with a shiny gold buckle on his head. His tiny buckled shoes were on the ground beside him. He was carrying something in his hand, and when Cormac looked at it closely he could see that it was an awl no bigger than a needle.

'This is my lucky day,' Cormac thought to himself. 'I have found a leprechaun and it's well known that every leprechaun has a pot of gold. If I don't let him out of my sight he will have to lead me to the gold and then it will be mine.'

Cormac grabbed the leprechaun. The little man struggled, but Cormac held him tightly while he released his beard from the bush. This made the leprechaun very angry, but Cormac ignored his oaths and curses and whistled a merry tune.

He knew that he mustn't lose sight of the leprechaun, so he kept a firm hold on him.

'Put me down!' the leprechaun shouted.

'Not until you tell me where your crock of gold is hidden,' replied Cormac.

For a long time the leprechaun refused to say anything, but finally he realised that Cormac wasn't going to let him go.

'Oh, all right then, I give up,' he said sulkily. 'The gold is buried under this bush. Now let me go.'

Cormac was delighted to have persuaded the leprechaun to give away his hiding place so easily, but then he realised that he wasn't carrying a spade with him.

'If I go home now, how will I remember which bush is the one with the gold buried underneath it? I'll have to take you with me.'

'No need for that,' said the wily leprechaun. 'Just tie your handkerchief to the bush to mark it.'

'That's a good idea,' agreed Cormac, forgetting that he was supposed to keep his eyes on the leprechaun until he found the gold, 'but you must promise not to take the gold while I'm gone.'

The leprechaun promised, so Cormac put him down, tied his red handkerchief to the lowest branch of the bush and set off home at top speed to fetch his spade.

By the time he got back to the bush dawn was breaking. As he got nearer, what a sight met his eyes. Every bush for miles around had a red handkerchief tied to its lowest branch.

'Oh no,' he groaned, 'what a fool I was to let the leprechaun out of my sight. I'll never find the gold now.'

He set off home, dragging his spade behind him.
Perhaps it was his imagination, but he thought he
could hear the sound of laughter blowing in the wind.

The Fairy Lios

One afternoon in May, Eithne and her brother Conor were playing in the field behind their house. Conor was playing the tin whistle that he always carried with him, while Eithne was busy making daisy chains for all her dolls. She decided to pick some of the lovely wildflowers that were growing all over the field to take home to her mother. Her favourites were bluebells, with their little helmet-shaped flowers.

She went further into the field, her bunch of bluebells growing as she moved along on her knees through the wildflower meadow.

'Don't pick any flowers from the fairy lios,' Conor warned. 'You know we've been told not to.'

Eithne ignored him and continued to pick bluebells from the centre of the lios.

'There are so many growing here that the fairies aren't going to notice if I pick a few,' she said.

At lunchtime the children went home and Eithne put the bluebells in a vase in the middle of the kitchen table. As soon as her mother heard that she had picked some of them in the lios, she rushed outside and put the vase on the window ledge. She knew that if the fairy people were angry with Eithne for picking their flowers, she would be punished for interfering with the lios. She hoped that taking the flowers out of the house would improve things for Eithne.

When Eithne got into bed that night she jumped up, screaming. Her bed was full of stinging nettles! She tried to sleep in her parents' bed, but as soon as she lay down it, too, was suddenly full of nettles. She even tried Conor's bed, but the same thing happened.

The next day, after a sleepless night, Eithne's parents went to visit a wise old woman who lived nearby.

'The fairies won't be easy to please,' she said, when she had heard the sorry tale. 'But if someone in your family could do a good deed for them, it might just persuade them to remove the nettles from your daughter's bed.'

No matter how hard the family thought about this, they couldn't think of anything that they could do for the fairies. At last, Conor had an idea. That very night, he crept out of the house and went to the lios.

By the time he got there it was midnight and little lights were twinkling all over the lios. He could hear

soft music playing. Conor loved music and he could play all sorts of tunes on his tin whistle. As he listened, he recognised some of the tunes and he thought to himself that it was very strange that the little people should have the same music as mortals.

He moved forward very cautiously and parted the bushes. Fairies and leprechauns were dancing merrily in the centre of the lios, their little lanterns hanging from the bluebells.

'That leprechaun has a tin whistle just like mine,' he thought. When the music stopped he moved forward. There was silence, then one of the leprechauns spoke.

'Your sister disturbed our lios and now you have come to disturb our dancing,' he said angrily.

'No, no,' said Conor, 'I have come to tell you how sorry she is and to promise that she will never do such a thing again. Please take the nettles from her bed and let her sleep.'

'That's impossible!' said the leprechaun. 'Go away before we punish you, too.'

The leprechaun turned to the musician.

'Let the music start again!' he ordered.

Conor stood outside the lios feeling very sad. He had failed and his sister would never be able to sleep again. Then, as the fairy music started again, he had another idea.

When the next dance was over and he thought that the musician was probably resting before the next set, he began to play a soft, sad tune on his whistle. He parted the bushes and stepped into the lios again, playing all the while. This time the fairy people listened.

Conor played for what seemed to be for ever. When he had finished, you could have heard a pin drop. Then the applause started. When it had finally died away, the leprechaun who had spoken earlier spoke again.

'Well played, Conor,' he said. 'You are a brave young man and we must reward you. Just tell us your wish and we will make it come true.'

'Oh no, I don't want anything for myself,' Conor said. 'I just want you to help my sister.'

The leprechaun turned to the others. They all nodded.

'Go home now,' said the leprechaun. 'We will grant your wish.'

At that moment dawn broke, and the fairies vanished in an instant.

Conor went straight home and found Eithne fast asleep in bed. His family knew that Conor had somehow broken the spell, but they also knew that they could never ask how.

As long as he lived Conor never told anyone about his night with the fairies.

The Sídhe

Once upon a time, the people of the village used to spend the winter evenings sitting at the fireside singing and telling stories. They would gather in a different house every night, so that everyone took their turn as host for the evening.

Seán loved these evenings – he was a great singer and he could tell as good a story as the next person, but unlike his family and his neighbours, he didn't believe in fairies or leprechauns or any of the little people. Whenever he heard anyone talk about the sídhe he would burst out laughing, saying that he couldn't understand how anyone could be so foolish as to believe that any of the stories could actually be true.

One warm summer's day, when winter was just

a distant memory, Seán was having a snooze at the edge of his field. The air was filled with the sounds of summer – birds were chirping and bees were humming as they moved from plant to plant, collecting pollen.

Suddenly, Seán woke up. He had been dreaming that he could hear another sound, a gentle tap-tapping, and when he was awake he could still hear it. It seemed to be coming from the nearby hedge. He moved forward very slowly to investigate.

Imagine his surprise when he saw a little man sitting on a mushroom, hard at work repairing shoes. All around him were pairs of tiny shoes, some with silver buckles, some dainty fairy slippers and a few pairs of hefty boots. Although he was right in front of him, Seán still couldn't believe that he was seeing a leprechaun, a real live one, just like those he had always said didn't exist. However, even though he had never believed in them, he had always enjoyed the stories. Now that he had a real one within his grasp, he knew just what he should do.

With the speed of lightning, he reached out and grabbed the little man.

'Where is your pot of gold?' he demanded.

'Gold?' said the little man crossly. 'Gold, is it? Where would I get a pot of gold? Sure, I'm only a poor cobbler, mending shoes to make a living. All I possess in the world are my cobbling tools and this little piece of leather.'

'You can't fool me,' said Seán. 'I know you have a pot of gold and I won't set you free until you give me your treasure.'

'All right, so,' said the leprechaun (for he really was a leprechaun), 'I'll show you where my gold is. It's buried in a field by the river. If you take me there I'll show you exactly where it is.'

Even though he didn't believe a word of them, Seán had listened carefully to the stories and he knew that if he was to get his hands on the gold, he couldn't take his eyes off the leprechaun for even an instant. He followed closely behind the little man as he led him across the fields to the water's edge.

'There you are,' said the leprechaun, pointing to a bush. 'There's my gold, yours for the taking.'

Keeping his eyes on the leprechaun, Seán reached into the bush . . . and screamed. Instead of grasping a pot of gold, he had put his hand into a beehive!

Naturally, he looked to where the bees were, and as soon as he had taken his eyes off the leprechaun, he disappeared, just as all the stories said he would.

Whenever it was Seán's turn to tell a story during the long winter nights, he never mentioned how he had been fooled by the leprechaun.

But no one ever again heard him say that he didn't believe in fairies or leprechauns.

Eisirt

During a feast, the king of the little people was boasting about his great strength and about how he was the greatest warrior alive when he noticed the expression on the face of his poet, Eisirt.

'Why are you looking at me like that?' demanded the king. 'Don't you believe that I'm the greatest warrior living today?'

'You're certainly the bravest warrior in our land,' said Eisirt, 'but beyond the hills there are men so tall that just one of them on his own could defeat our army and kill all our people.'

The king was furious and gave Eisirt five days and five nights to prove that these giants really existed.

Eisirt knew he had a problem: if he didn't return with proof the king would probably have him killed; on the other hand, if he succeeded in finding the giants they would very likely save the king the trouble by killing him themselves.

He set out to find the evidence he needed. After two days and two nights on the road he reached the palace of King Fergus of Ulster. A feast was being held in honour of the king in the great hall.

Terrified, Eisirt walked up to the guard and demanded to be let in. The guard laughed at the tiny man, but then he opened the door and let him in. All the guests rushed over to see Eisirt.

'Stay away from me, you great monsters!' he roared. But all the people heard was a little squeak, like that of a mouse.

Eisirt saw a dwarf (this was Conn, Fergus's chief poet) and said, 'I will speak to this small giant.'

Conn reached down, lifted Eisirt and placed him on the table in front of the king.

'Who are you, little man, and where do you come from?' asked the king.

'I am Eisirt, chief poet and wise man of my people,' said Eisirt proudly.

'You are every welcome here,' said Fergus. 'You must join us for the feast and after you have eaten you must sing for us and tell us about your home.'

The king called for a seat for Eisirt and ordered food and drink for him. This was easier said than done. Where would they find a seat small enough for the little man, and from what could he possibly drink? All the goblets were far too big. The queen came up with the solution, giving Eisirt her golden thimble to drink from and her brooch to sit on.

'Sit and enjoy yourself, poet,' said the king. 'You have come a long way and you must be very hungry and thirsty.'

'I will not drink your wine or eat your food!' shouted Eisirt.

There was silence in the great hall, and all the courtiers held their breath, for nobody had ever spoken to the king in this way.

Suddenly the king laughed.

'Oh dear,' he said. 'Why are you so angry with me? If I am not careful you might challenge me to a duel, and what chance would I have against bravery such as yours? I will put you in my goblet and then you will have to drink.'

With that, the king lifted Eisirt and dropped him into a goblet of wine. The little man tried to swim, but he soon became tired and knew that he would drown if no one rescued him.

'King Fergus of Ulster!' he cried. 'You are doing a foolish thing. If I drown you will never hear about my wonderful home or where it is.'

'Save him! Save him!' everyone cried, for they loved a good story and they felt sure that the little man had an interesting one to tell.

Fergus took him out and dried him off.

'Why did you insult us by refusing our kind hospitality?' he asked.

'If I told you,' said Eisirt, 'you would be very angry with me and I don't think that people who make you angry live very long.'

'I give you my word that I will listen to what you say and that you will not be harmed,' answered the king.

'Well,' said Eisirt, 'I cannot stand injustice and I know that you are unjust to your chief steward. I cannot eat or drink here while this is happening.'

There was silence once again in the hall. This was treason! No one spoke to the king like this and got away with it.

Then the king spoke.

'You are a strange little man with strange powers indeed. I do not know how you understand these things, for you have only just arrived in our land. It is true. I have been unfair to my chief steward, but I will put things right immediately.'

'Sir,' replied Eisirt, 'there is nothing worse than an unjust king, but there is nothing better than a king who admits that he is unjust and promises to change. Now I will join your feast.'

Eisirt sat down on the brooch again, lifted the thimble and drank the wine. The courtiers listened long into the night as he told them wonderful stories about his people and about the land from where he had come and why.

The next morning, the queen gave Eisirt her thimble so that he could prove to his countrymen that tall men really did exist. Eisirt put it in a bag so that he could carry it on his back and he travelled home again, arriving just before the five days and five nights were up. When he showed his ruler the thimble the king knew that Eisirt had been speaking the truth, and he

marvelled that there were people with fingers so big
that they would need such a large thimble.

The king pardoned Eisirt, although he was now a
little worried to have discovered that his kingdom was
so close to a kingdom of giants.

The Huntsman's Son

Along, long time ago a huntsman and his wife and son, Fergus, lived in a little house in the forest. Fergus used to hunt with his father in the forest and he grew up as strong and as swift-footed as a deer, and as free and fearless as the wind. He never wanted to leave the forest, until one winter's night a wandering minstrel took shelter with the family and sang songs of famous battles. Ever since, Fergus had pined for the life of a warrior and he spent all his spare time learning how to use weapons and practising the harp, for in those days the bravest warriors were also bards. A year later there was a fierce storm one night.

After being woken by a loud clap of thunder, Fergus heard three knocks at the door.

'Open the door at once,' said his father. 'This is no night to keep a poor wanderer outside.'

As Fergus opened the door a flash of lightning lit up a little old man with a small harp under his arm.

'Come in and welcome,' said Fergus, and the little man stepped into the room.

The huntsman's wife lit the fire and brought the old man a jug of milk and some bread.

'While you're eating, sir, I'll make up a bed for you,' she said.

'Don't go to any trouble,' said the little man. 'I can sleep by the fire.'

'It's no trouble at all,' said the good woman, 'but I'll leave you to sleep by the fire if you'd prefer that. Goodnight now and sleep well.'

'Goodnight,' said the little man. 'Maybe some time when you won't be expecting it I'll do a good turn for your kindness to a poor wayfarer.'

The family went back to their beds and were soon fast asleep.

After about an hour another clap of thunder woke Fergus again and he heard three loud knocks at the door. He opened the door and a flash of lightning lit up a little old woman with a shuttle under her arm.

'Come in and welcome,' he said, and the woman stepped into the room. The huntsman's wife offered the old woman food and drink and a bed for the night, and then she went back to bed.

About an hour later another clap of thunder startled Fergus. Again he heard three knocks at the door. On the threshold he saw a small, wild-looking horse with flames coming from its nostrils. He knew at once that it was the pooka, the wild horse of the mountains.

'Come in and welcome,' he said, and the horse was treated as hospitably as the old man and woman had been earlier that evening.

Soon, everyone in the house was fast asleep again.

When the morning came the sun was shining through the windows of the hut. When Fergus got up, there was no sign of any of the visitors to the house.

About a week later Fergus told his parents he wanted to join the Fianna and he set out for the high king's palace at Tara. He arrived there just at a time when the great captain of the Fianna was recruiting.

In order to be accepted into the Fianna, Fergus had to prove that he could play the harp like a bard, fight against nine Fenian warriors, run through the tangled forest without losing a single hair, jump over trees as high as his head and run so lightly that rotten twigs would not break under his feet. Fergus passed all the tests, thanks to the wandering minstrel who taught him to play the harp, to his own brave heart, and to his forest training. He was enrolled in the Fianna and before long he was its bravest champion.

At that time the high king's beautiful niece was staying at the palace at Tara. She had suitors from all over the world, but she had vowed she would marry no one except a battle champion who could surpass the high king's chief bard in music; who could run faster on his horse in the great race of Tara than the white horse of the plains; and who could give her a wedding dress of all the colours of the rainbow, so finely spun that it would fit in the palm of her hand.

When Fergus saw the princess he fell head over heels in love with her but knew that his love was hopeless.

The great fair of Tara was coming up, and all the Fianna were practising from morning to night. Fergus, knowing that the princess would be present, was determined to do his best to win all the prizes.

On the first day of the fair, at a signal from the high king, the champions poised their spears, and at a stroke from the heralds on their shields the spears sped through the air. When they hit the ground, shafts up, two stood side by side ahead of the rest. One belonged to Fergus, the other to the great chief, Oscar. When Fergus threw his spear a full length ahead of Oscar's, the air was shaken by a wild cheer. The princess was almost sorry for her vow, for she had taken a fancy to the handsome Fenian champion.

Fergus went into the forest feeling very sad because he knew he could never win the princess. Suddenly, he heard a noise behind him, and who should he see but the little old man who had found shelter in his father's home on the stormy night.

'This is a nice place for a battle champion to be on the day which is to decide who will be the successful suitor of the princess,' said the old man.

'What is it to me?' said Fergus. 'I cannot win her.'

'I told you,' said the little man, 'that I might be able to do a good turn for you and yours. The time has come. Take this harp, and my luck go with you.'

The little man handed his harp to Fergus and disappeared. Fergus hid the harp under his cloak and got back to the camp at dawn, just before his comrades woke up.

When the time came for the great contest to start the chief bard ascended the mound, and at the first note of his harp silence fell. When his last notes had died away a great cheer arose. Then it was the turn of the bard from the northern lands. When he had finished a great shout went up. Then Fergus got ready to play. All eyes were fastened upon him, but no one was watching as eagerly as the princess.

Fergus touched his harp with gentle fingers, and when he had stopped playing there was complete silence, for the audience was spellbound. Although he was declared the winner, he was sad, because the great race was the next day and he knew that his horse couldn't compete with the white horse of the plains.

He passed the night in the forest without sleep, and when the morning came he arose and walked aimlessly through the woods.

Suddenly, he saw the wild horse of the mountains standing before him.

'I owe you a good turn,' said the pooka. 'You have no time to lose. The white steed of the plains is coming to the starting post. Jump on my back.'

Just as the king was about to declare that there was no steed to compete with the white horse of the plains, the pooka galloped up to the royal enclosure with Fergus on his back. When the people saw the champion a thunderous shout rose up. At the striking of the shields the two horses rushed from the post. But before the white steed of the plains had reached the halfway stage, Fergus and the pooka had passed the winning post, greeted by such cheers as had never before been heard on the plains of Tara.

And the princess was truly sorry for her vow, for she

didn't think Fergus could bring her a rainbow-coloured robe, so subtly woven as to fit in the palm of her hand.

That night Fergus went to the forest again. When morning came he was not surprised when the little old woman with the shuttle appeared.

'Go and pick me a handful of wild forest flowers,' she said. 'I'll weave a wedding robe for the princess.'

Fergus gathered the flowers, and in the twinkling of an eye the old woman wove a rainbow-coloured robe as light as the fairy dew and so small that it would pass through the eye of a needle.

Fergus took the robe and went to Tara and rode up to the queen's pavilion. Holding up the robe, he said:

'I claim the princess for my bride. I have won all the prizes and it is for the princess to say if this robe will fit in the palm of her hand.'

The princess took the robe from Fergus and closed her fingers over it.

'Yes!' she exclaimed. 'He has fulfilled the final condition of the vow I made; but before he had fulfilled even one of them, my heart had gone out to the handsome champion of the Fianna. I was willing then and I am ready now to become the bride of Fergus, the huntsman's son.'

The Golden Spear

Along, long time ago an old fisherman and his son, Rory, lived in the middle of a lake in a little house built on stilts. The only way the fisherman and Rory could leave their house was in their currach, which they kept moored to a little wooden platform attached to the house.

Rory often lay on the platform on summer evenings, watching the sun setting in the mountains and the twilight creeping over the waters of the lake. One night, as he lay stretched out on the platform, he heard rustling. He turned to where the sound came from, and what should he see but an otter swimming towards him with a little trout in his mouth. The otter lifted his head and half his body from the water, flung the trout on the platform at Rory's feet and disappeared. Rory picked up the panting trout, but he felt sorry for the little creature, so he threw it back into the water.

As soon as the trout touched the water it was transformed into a beautiful, milk-white swan and it swam elegantly to the edge of the lake and disappeared into the rushes.

The next day, Rory got into his currach and rowed all around the shore of the lake, beating the rushes with his oar, looking for the swan. Day after day he rowed around the lake looking for her, and every evening he lay on the platform watching the waters. At long last, one night, when the full moon had flooded the whole lake with light, he saw the swan coming towards him. Soon she was within a boat's length of the hut.

'Get into your currach, Rory, and follow me,' she said, then she turned around and swam away.

Rory jumped into the currach and rowed after the swan. When she came to the deepest part of the lake she stopped and Rory drew level with her.

'Who are you?' he asked.

'I am Princess Maeve, the daughter of the king,' she replied. 'My cruel stepmother cast a spell to change me into a trout, and she threw me into the lake. Because you threw me back, I have been turned into a swan, and for one hour on the first night of every full moon I will have the power of speech. But I will always be a swan, unless you are willing to break the enchantment; and only you can break it.'

'But how can I break the spell?' asked Rory.

'You can only do so,' said the swan, 'by pouring

on my plumage the perfumed water in a golden bowl that is to be found in the innermost room of the fairy queen's palace, which lies beneath the lake.'

'And how can I get that?' said Rory, wondering what he had let himself in for, but deciding that he would do anything to free a beautiful princess.

'You must dive beneath the lake,' said the swan, 'and walk along the lake bed, until you come to where the lake dragon guards the entrance to the fairy queen's palace.'

'I can dive like a fish,' said Rory, 'but how can I walk beneath the waters?'

'You can do it easily enough if you wear the tunic and crystal helmet that you will find under the first rock you see when you dive down into the waters. You must be quick, though,' added the swan. 'If the spell is not broken before the next full moon, it cannot be broken for another year and a day. The hours of silence are coming upon me now, and I have only time to warn you that your quest for the golden cup will put you in great danger.'

The swan sailed away to the banks of the lake and disappeared.

Rory rowed home and went to bed, but was so agitated by everything that had happened that he didn't get any sleep that night. As soon as dawn broke, he rowed to the deepest part of the lake and dived in.

When he reached the bed of the lake he saw a large rock. As soon as he approached it a dozen fairy nymphs swam up from underneath it, carrying a tunic, a crystal helmet and a shining golden spear. They laid them at Rory's feet and then disappeared. He put on the tunic and the helmet and then picked up the spear. As he did so he heard a musical voice tinkling in his ears.

'The tunic and the helmet will enable you to walk under the water,' he heard. 'If you use the spear with courage you can overcome everything and everyone that tries to stop you.'

Rory began to walk along the lake bed. He had not gone very far when he heard a horrible hissing. He took a few more steps and found himself face to face with the dragon of the lake, the guardian of the palace of the fairy queen. Before he had time to raise his spear, the dragon had wound its coils around him, and he heard its horrible teeth crunching against the side of his crystal helmet. The breath almost left his body, but the dragon couldn't pierce the helmet and he unwound his coils. As soon as Rory's hands were free, he drove his spear through one of the dragon's eyes. The dragon backed away, hissing loudly, and Rory went on his way until he came to a brass door in the rocks. There was no handle but he touched the door with the point of his spear and it flew open.

The door closed behind him with a grating sound and Rory found himself on top of a huge, jagged rock. In front of him, just across a small plain, was another rock, guarded by a monster with huge bloodshot eyes. Rory threw his spear with all his might between the monster's eyes, killing him instantly, then he climbed down from the rock and walked across the plain to a little wood. He had not gone far into the wood when he heard the sound of fairy music, and soon came upon some tiny, brightly dressed fairies, dancing around their queen.

'You are welcome, Rory,' said the queen. 'I know what you have come for. You will have the golden cup tomorrow, but tonight you must share our feast.'

The queen set off through the wood, with Rory and the fairies following, and soon they arrived at a beautiful crystal palace. They went into a large banqueting hall, lit by a huge single star that was fixed to the wall above a sparkling diamond throne.

The queen sat down on the throne and waved her golden wand three times. A table laden with all kinds of food appeared. Then she beckoned Rory to her. She tapped him with her wand and he became small enough to sit at the table with all the nobles of the court.

When everyone was eating and drinking the queen ordered the harpists to play. Rory felt as if he was being slowly lifted from his seat, and when the music ended the fairies vanished, the shining star went out and he was left in complete darkness.

He could feel cool air on his face, and at last he saw a faint grey light. Imagine his surprise when he found himself lying in his currach on the lake in the moonlight, with the tunic, crystal helmet and golden spear beside him, together with a golden bowl full of perfumed water.

Swimming towards him from the bank came the beautiful swan. When she touched the boat Rory lifted her in and poured the perfumed water from the golden bowl over her plumage. There was a flash of light and a beautiful princess stood before him.

'Row to the lakeside,' she said, and Rory, dazzled by her beauty, did as she asked.

'Now set your boat adrift with the tunic and helmet, but keep the spear,' said the princess. They both walked together until they came to a forest where they came upon a hunt. The hunt had driven a wild boar towards them and it was about to attack them. Rory pushed the princess behind him and drove his spear into the beast's throat. It fell dead at his feet just as the huntsmen arrived, led by the king, who immediately recognised his daughter, Princess Maeve.

'I thought you were dead,' said the king, 'but here you are, more lovely than ever. I would gladly have given up my throne for this. But who is this champion who has brought you here, and has killed the wild boar we have hunted so many years in vain?'

'His name is Rory, Father,' replied the princess, blushing like a rose.

The king invited Rory to the palace to a great feast in thanksgiving for his daughter's safe return.

As soon as they arrived at the palace, the king's wicked wife fell down and died from the shock of seeing her step-daughter restored. The king had no idea until then that she had placed his daughter under a spell. As soon as Maeve told him about her enchantment and how Rory had rescued her, the king offered him his daughter's hand in marriage.

Rory accepted immediately and the princess almost fainted with happiness. There was rejoicing throughout the realm when the marriage of the princess and her brave champion took place.

Pronunciation Guide

Irish names and words can look very strange, with lots of silent consonants and accents on vowels. To complicate things, some words are pronounced differently depending on which region of Ireland the speaker comes from. This handy phonetic guide will show you how the words you come across in this book are usually pronounced.

Ailill	*Al-ill*
Aodh	*Ey*
Aoife	*Ee-fah*
Bobdal	*Bub-dol*
Brian Bóruma	*Bree-an Bur-oo-ah*
Caoilte Mac Rónáin	*Queelta Mock Roh-nawn*

Caomhóg	*Quee-vogue*
Cathbad	*Ca-bod*
Chogaidh	*Cugga*
Conán Maol	*Cun-awn Mweel*
Cormac Mac Airt	*Cor-mock Mock Art*
Cúchulainn	*Coo-cullen*
Culann	*Cullen*
currach	*curr-ock*
Dagda	*Dowda*
Daire	*Dara*
Dál Cais	*Dall Cash*
Deirdre	*Deer-drah*
Diarmuid	*Deer-mwid*
Eisirt	*Esh-urt*

Eithne	*Eth-na*
Eoin	*Owen*
Fiacal	*Fee-ack-al*
Fiachra	*Fee-ack-ra*
Fianna	*Fee-anna*
Finnbhennach	*Finn-ven-ock*
Finnéigeas	*Finn-ey-gas*
Fionn Mac Cumhaill	*Finn Mock-Cool*
Fionnuala	*Finn-oola*
Gleann Máma	*Glown Mawma*
Gleann na Smól	*Glown na Smole*
Gráinne	*Graw-nyeh*
Granuaile	*Graw-nyeh-wale*
Howth	*Hoath*

Labhra	*La-owera*
Leabharcham	*La-owercom*
lios	*liss*
Macra	*Mock-ra*
Maeve	*Mave*
moruadh	*muh-roo-ah*
Naoise	*Neesha*
Niamh	*Nee-uv*
Samhain	*Sa-ow-un*
sídhe	*shee*
Sliabh Bloom	*Shleeve Bloom*
Tír na nÓg	*Tier-na-Nogue*
Tuatha Dé Danann	*Too-aha Day Donnan*
Uisneach	*Ish-nock*